NATIR

WHITEBRIDGE

Book II
Dog Cage

By
James Starvoice

CONTENTS

ACKNOWLEDGMENT

My gratitude to the best editor in the world,

Stephanie Hoogstad

despite battling with migraine pain throughout
the whole project, her hard work, dedication, and
remarkable talent have given this book the most
perfected shape it can possibly have,

Stephanie, your contribution to this work is simply priceless.
Thank you,

James Starvoice

Chapter 1

MYSTIC

She tried not to look suspicious as she pretended to take a casual walk in the middle of the night.

Dirty snow caught the ends of her woolen dress as she strolled down the trail surrounded by tents, fires, and the occasional harlots' laughter resounding in the dark.

She joined her hands behind her back and tilted her head towards the stars, putting extra effort into avoiding the looks of the few men she passed and any unnecessary conversation it may spark until she was a tent away from her intended target: the tall, dark-green tent next to the great sessile-oak.

Natir stopped and toyed at a rock with her foot while she waited for the two men carrying a pot between them to pass. Once they were gone, she stole looks left and right then hurried round to the back of the tent, pulled up the heavy cover, and snuck inside.

She was still on her arms and knees, half tucked inside, when the naughty smile on her face quickly vanished.

Alfred lay on his back right in front of her with Agatha, as bare before Natir's eyes as the day she was born, mounting him.

All three of them froze with momentous awkwardness.

"What are you doing here?" Agatha breathed fire on her lips.

"Um...sorry...I—"

"OUT!"

Natir retreated in a hurry.

"You little bitch, wait 'til I get my hands on you! Who sneaks up on people like that?"

Natir wasn't sure what Agatha threw at her, but the impact it made against the tent's cover made her feel grateful it missed her head.

She wiped her face with her palms to try and efface the disturbing image from her mind. She cursed her luck and headed back to her wagon, grunting with jealousy and venting her wrath on every mound of snow in her way.

"The bitch!" Natir climbed inside.

Her companions who shared her wagon, Volk and Teyrnon, raised their heads from where they lay. Teyrnon moved the oil lamp they had hung to the ceiling to reveal the scene.

Natir blew her huffs left and right while she wrestled her shoes off and mumbled unintelligible curses.

"I swear...one of these days...straight to the face...she won't see it coming...she won't."

She managed to hang her shoes after several failed attempts and made her way inside. Fur covered the wagon's floor underneath her puttees-wrapped feet.

Volk dared to ask, "Who are we talking about again?"

"Agatha, who else?"

"What did she do?" Teyrnon asked.

Natir sat at her spot and looked away, biting her fist.

He asked again, "What happened?"

She shouted, "She's such a quiet fuck, that's what happened. The bitch can have the orgasm of her life two steps away from a dog, and it still won't hear a thing!"

"Oh!" Teyrnon chuckled.

Volk lay back down and pulled the cover over his head. "Do the smart thing: Give up."

"Don't listen to him, Natir. You only need to wait for the right chance."

"What chance?" Natir burst out. "Does it look like she's giving me a chance? She's following him closer than his own shadow."

Teyrnon shrugged. "Just wait for the right chance."

Volk said, "If you need it so badly, you're welcome to share my blanket."

"Do you ever stop being gross?" Natir waved her arm and looked away.

Teyrnon shook his head. "You're being too hard on yourself." She didn't respond. He pushed himself closer to her without letting go of his blanket. "It's all about the right timing, and you will get your chance sooner than you think," he said softly.

"How?" she squeaked. "We're on the move most of the time, and Agatha is all over him every hour of the day." She dropped her face. "It's been days...I can't even have a word alone with him anymore. I didn't think it would be like this."

Volk chuckled. "What, you thought he'd be calling you to

his tent every night or something?"

"Do yourself a favor, Volk, and shut up!"

"Natir, look, it's not what you think of it, really," Teyrnon said. "It's just what Agatha does. We're used to it. You know, we think nothing of it anymore. She has a habit of getting unreasonably wary over Alfred at times like these. But you know what else? Even Agatha can't watch him all day long."

"She can."

"No, she can't. At least not *everywhere*," Teyrnon teased and increased the intensity of the lamp's light, which caused Natir to finally meet his gaze.

"Did you forget already? We'll be arriving to Wenclas tomorrow," Teyrnon said with a wink, but Natir remained silent. "What? Don't tell me you don't know what that means?"

"She probably never heard of it."

"You've never heard of Wenclas? Really?"

Clueless and irritated, she shrugged.

"Oh. Well then, no wonder you don't know what I'm talking about. It's a town, just beyond the hills—"

Volk joined the conversation, caroling with his eyes shut and hoping to sound poetic, "Oh, tactful Wenclas, you're a carpet weaved of men's dreams."

Natir turned her face between them as they spoke.

"It's ten times larger than any village you've been to—"

"Twenty times larger."

"Built overnight, on top of a river."

She raised an eyebrow. "Did you say on top of it?"

"The river god holds it in place," Volk said. "It's the only good thing the gods ever did."

"Gold is spent there like bronze, and wine is spilled like water."

"The things they have, the food, and the women—"

"All right, all right, I get it," she said. "So, it's a great place. What does that have to do with what we were talking about?"

Teyrnon explained, "Well, it's also the largest trade hub around. There is nothing like it for tens of miles, and not a single merchant doesn't have to go through it as it sits over the only road connecting these parts together. So, when an earl just so happens to pass by Wenclas, what do you think he will do?"

She shrugged. "What? He will probably stop to do—" It suddenly dawned on her, causing Natir to hop with excitement, "BUSINESS! He will stop to trade. He won't miss the chance."

"Now you get it. And he can't do that with a passionate bodyguard following him all over the place, can he? I mean, what will the merchants think of him?"

Volk said, "No one but the town guards can carry weapons in Wenclas, anyway. So, what does Agatha got to worry about? He will tell her to get off his back and leave him alone."

She yelped, "When do we get there?"

"Tomorrow at the latest," Teyrnon said. "So, you see, it's just like I told you: all that you need is to seize the right chance to be alone with him. And, also," he added with a devious grin, "I just so happen to know this *special place*. They'll take care of you."

His tone alerted her. She raised an eyebrow. "What...take care of me?"

"Don't worry," he winked, "I'm paying."

*   *   *

A servant stood with her back to the wall, next to a shut door.

Her hand had gotten wearied from holding the oil lamp, so she set it down and sat on the floor, waiting with a troubled expression on her face.

Soon enough, the sound of footsteps down the shadowy corridor stole her eyes. She saw that her friend, holding another lamp, had returned with the keeper.

She straightened up with no hurry.

Although the keeper held a prestigious place, there were hardly any formalities among the three women who had known each other for years and were the only ones allowed to live in this guarded residence that was forbidden to most.

The keeper, Alediya, sure was someone to look up to; she was an older woman with an authoritarian attitude and a very keen eye. She was sharp of mind and very strong for her age and firm when she needed to be but treated them fairly and with kindness.

"She refuses to get any sleep," the servant said, certain that her friend had already explained it all.

"How long has this been going on?" asked Alediya.

"It's the third night in a row."

"You can tell she's exhausted from lack of sleep," her friend added. "Alediya, we offered her potions and said everything we can think of to try and convince her, but she refuses to listen—"

"Then you should have called for me sooner," the keeper interrupted, causing the others to drop their faces.

Alediya reached out her hand to the servant, who gave her a bottle with a sleeping potion.

"I'll handle this. You two wait here."

Alediya entered the room and shut the door behind her. She saw the Mystic, Hallstein, sitting on her bed, staring out the window with her back to Alediya.

The candles' light highlighted Hallstein's side. It reflected beautifully on her perfect skin and loose silver hair, making her delicate figure almost visible through her thin clothes.

"Hallstein…" Alediya called softly.

Hallstein's little motion was rather slow with fatigue but sensuous as she looked back at Alediya, her fair face soiled with tiredness.

"What's wrong, my dear?"

Hallstein's face fell. "Nothing."

"Nothing?" Alediya came closer. "They tell me you have not slept in three days. I would never consider such a serious thing to be nothing if it came from a normal woman…" She held Hallstein's chin and made her look up at her. "But, of all people, for it to come from you, I certainly can't overlook it as *nothing*."

Hallstein looked away. "But I am a normal woman."

Alediya sat next to her. "You know what I meant, my dear." She threw her arm around Hallstein and massaged her shoulder. "What, do you really want me to see you on the same level as other people? On the same level as the servants and the commoners? *Never.* Not in my eyes. You are beyond normal. You are beyond wonderful. You are one and only."

"No. Just normal is fine. Just normal is all I wish for."

Alediya sighed and embraced her. "Why do you talk like this? Do you wish to break this old woman's heart with that sad tone of yours?"

Hallstein hugged her back. "Alediya, you're not old."

"That's what I tell myself every morning, but when I open my door, where have all my young lovers gone?" she humored, causing Hallstein to chuckle. "Well, it's not like I'm being greedy or anything. Just two or three fine young men with some muscle in their lower backs are all I'm asking for."

"*Two or three?*" She laughed.

"What are you laughing at? Believe me, this old goat can still surprise you." Alediya looked away with a pretended sigh. "But I guess my pouch of luck must have long ran out. Now, the only man I got chasing my old robes is Helmut the greenskeeper, and his face is worse than my sandal stuck in a bull's ass."

"*Eww*, you and Helmut?"

"Oh, you've seen him before?"

"Only from the window."

"Morana bless your eyes, don't look too close. You'll go blind."

Hallstein cracked a laugh.

"But enough about me, love," said Alediya. "Why don't you tell me what troubles your night instead?"

Hallstein dropped her face. The gloom blemished her expression once again, and after a little pause, she answered under her breath, "Alediya, I had a dream."

"Just *one* dream?"

She shook her head. "No. It came to me more than once."

"Oh, I see. The world has spoken to you again?" she asked. Hallstein nodded. "But then, why didn't you send for me?"

"Because…" Hallstein's slender fingers tightened over the sheets.

"Did it frighten you?" she asked. Hallstein nodded in response.

Alediya turned Hallstein's face towards her and brushed the silver bangs from over her face. "Well, you've got no reason to be afraid anymore. I'm here now. So, why don't you tell me about it?"

She squeaked, "I can't."

"Darling, it's okay. Open up the gardens in your heart and let me be the confidante you are to me. Let me shoulder its weight with you."

"But—"

"Tell you what, I've got an idea. How about you start from the beginning and we'll walk through it together," Alediya said as she placed her hand over Hallstein's and held it tightly. "You will not have to go through it alone. I promise, I'll be right here with you every step of the way. So, what do you say, hm? You want to give it a try?"

Hallstein hesitated, but then she nodded again.

"All right then, take your time. Whenever you're ready."

Hallstein inhaled deeply through her nose, shut her eyes, and let it out. "It started a few days ago. It was terrible. I told myself that it was just a bad dream. I told myself that it meant nothing. But then, it kept coming back. For four nights, every time I fell asleep, I saw it happening all over again."

"What was it that you saw?"

"It's..it's myself I see… I'm in a shelter, but it looks weird, almost like a tent in the wild. Its fabric is thin, and I can see right through it. It's..it's not clear. The image is vague, as if someone is trying to hide the scenery from me, but I can still perceive what is it that I'm looking at… It's dark outside. So very dark. Perun is restless. Something has angered him. He has released the thunder-birds from the holy cage, and unbound, they flit through the sky, and there's a strong wind blowing from all around me. Storm-bound wind. And it's causing the trees to budge like the shadows of death. Alediya, Alediya, I'm afraid. I really don't want to remember."

"Hush," Alediya embraced her, "it's all right, it's all right. I'm right here, child. Was that what startled you, my dear?"

"No," she panted, "no, that's, that's not what I… Alediya, there's something else out there. Something monstrous is approaching. I can't see what it is, but I just know it's there, and it's frightening me. I'm so afraid. In my own dream, I'm afraid. I want to run, but I can't. My legs. I see my legs turn to wood like the trunk of a tree, their roots are in the ground, and I cannot run. And when I raise my face again… That's when I saw it."

"Saw what?"

"A shadow. A shadow so great, it can devour the world. It's moving slowly, right at the edge of my shelter. I..I can't breathe. I'm afraid to breathe. I've never felt anything so frightening in my life, and all that I want is for it to just go away and not see me… It's by the great willow tree now, the staff of Veles, shepherd of the worlds, and he ushers it away… It has passed. I see it move away. The shadow is almost gone. I'm safe. I'm safe and I can breathe again. No. It's looking back. It's looking right back at me, ALEDIYA!"

She screamed, prompting Alediya to wrap her arms tightly around the panicked woman, holding Hallstein's head to her chest.

"I'm here. I'm right here for you, and I will never let go. Easy now, *easy*…" she soothed. Alediya then faked a laugh as Hallstein whimpered with terror in her arms. "Oh, child, what a delicate soul you are. Is this the thief who stole sleep from your eyes?"

She stammered, "Alediya, you don't understand. I…I saw it. It looked back at me, and I saw what it was."

Hallstein raised her face and stared up at Alediya with desperate eyes, her trembling hands refusing to let go of Alediya's dress.

"It was a wolf. A wolf in chains. And the chains are breaking. And its eyes were the entirety of all the hate in the world."

The fear in her voice struck a nerve in her listener. It took

Alediya a moment to regain her soothing act.

"Now, you listen to me, dove," Alediya said kindly but with a motherly firmness, "I understand why you've been so troubled. But you need to know that what you fear has already passed. It's gone. It has been dealt with, and we're all perfectly safe, as you can see for yourself."

"Has it really?"

"Of course. That was but the army of Lord Valdes that you saw in your dream. Oh, what a vile horde of beasts and savages they are. Filth to my eyes. But by the grace and wisdom of our lord, they were dealt with, and we sent them off as friends. So, you see, you've got nothing to worry about."

"How...how do you know? What if it's something else? What if it's yet to come and—"

"That is but your tiredness speaking now," said Alediya. "You have exhausted yourself to the point that your lack of sleep is tampering with your judgment. Trust me, I've seen it happen before so many times, to so many good women. Once you get some proper rest…" She brought out the bottle with the sleeping potion and showed it to Hallstein. "Your mind shall know peace again, and you won't be thinking like that anymore… Take it, my dear. Let sleep hold your hand. It will make you feel so much better."

Her eyes to the bottle, Hallstein reached out her hand but hesitated and looked up at Alediya again. "You really believe that's what it was?"

She placed the bottle in Hallstein's hand, and gently closed her fingers over it. "With all my heart."

*   *   *

After Alediya had laid Hallstein to sleep, she stepped out of the room and glared at the two servants whom she caught eavesdropping at the door.

She walked past them, opened a window, and stared outside.

"Who's attending her needs tonight?" Alediya asked.

"I am."

"She should be out of it all night. Nevertheless, I want you to sleep in the bedroom, close to her bed, and if anything happens, you will report to me at once."

"Yes."

The other servant asked, "What do you think it means?"

Alediya glanced at her from over her shoulder. "Hallstein's dreams are no prophecies. Her perception of the world is different from ours, that's all." She turned towards them. "She is sensing a disturbance, and it's distorting her senses. Nothing more, nothing less."

"Yes, but…"

"You really think it was Lord Valdes's army that caused it?"

"I'm certain of it," Alediya said. "At least, I can't think of anything else of such magnitude, and the timing is also right."

A servant dropped her face and said under her breath, "She'd seen dark dreams before, but nothing that made her feel like this."

Alediya summoned a smile. "Cheer up. The storms have always surrounded Wenclas, and we overcome them every time. Besides, even if Hallstein's perception proved true and that what she saw is something yet to come, still, according to her own words, all that we need to do is to stay put and do nothing, and the storm will pass all on its own."

Alediya's gaze returned to the world outside.

"Nevertheless, the lord must be informed of this at once," she said firmly, watching the fire-illuminated bustling streets of the magnificent town. "Wenclas is more than our home. It is the foundation and future of our race. To secure its survival, we will turn the world upside-down and defy the gods themselves, if we have to… Nothing must stand in the way of Wenclas."

Chapter 2

PAYMENT

By the next sunset, the cries to raise the banners sounded along the column, signaling their approach of a settlement.

Towards an angry dark-gray sky illumed by the setting sun, the black-and-red banners of the Toic with two bulls' heads, painted as though they were charging at one another, rose once more, flapping with the wind and sending what few carriages and travelers were on the road scrambling out of the column's way.

Natir pushed the cover of her wagon, eager to have a look.

Her eyes glittered with astonishment.

It was a rarity to the world; the dense forest opened to a long road paved with stones and daily cleared from snow by herds of slaves. At the mouth of the road, there was a bridge wide enough for two wagons to pass side by side. It connected both sides of the swift river through an oval-shaped rocky island, on top of which sat the great trading town Wenclas.

Its walls were at least fifteen feet high, made of worked tree trunks and topped with watch towers, and were arrayed by a layer of frost making them look like they were made of a single piece of marble; the walls encircled the island end to end, not wasting an inch of the precious space, until it seemed to the beholders' eyes as though Wenclas had emerged from the river itself.

The gate they passed through was fit for a fortress. Three portcullises guarded the entrance, built only feet apart from one another. They were made of a foot-wide ironwood and reinforced with precious iron joints and heavy bronze, triple-decked watch towers on either side.

Once inside, a maze of paved narrow alleys lined with buildings welcomed Natir's eyes.

The clay-and-wood buildings stood three and even four stories high and were crammed closely together, as if they were fighting over space. Bronze fire-pits illuminated the streets from end to end.

Teyrnon patted Natir's shoulder and signaled her to follow him. They both jumped off the wagon as it was still moving.

"Hey, where are you going?" Volk called from the Waggoner's seat.

"Keep going, we'll catch up with you later."

"What?"

"I said keep going," Teyrnon yelled louder.

From where he stood, behind Natir, Teyrnon suddenly pulled Natir's cape over her head.

Surprised, Natir exclaimed, "Hey!"

"Keep it on."

"What? Why?"

"Just do as I tell you and keep it on. Now, let's go."

"Won't you at least tell me where we're going?"

"Don't worry, follow me."

She huffed, fixed her hood more comfortably, and made her way after him through the crowd.

Natir wasn't used to such overpopulated places and had some difficulty trying not to lose sight of Teyrnon. Everywhere she looked, people bustled, conducting their business at such a late hour in a town that never knew the taste of sleep and stores that never shut their doors.

It wasn't just the crowd that threatened to separate them but also all the new and fantastic things stealing her eyes left and right about every other step.

It was like drifting through a sinful dream.

Gamblers throwing coins like stones. Drunks celebrating naked in the streets. Children pushing carts or carrying baskets of merchandise Natir didn't even have a name for, racing to deliver the sales. Booths selling foods unlike any Natir had tasted before and that looked and smelled so good, they turned her mouth watery.

In the middle of the road, a lively woman danced with danger as she leapt and swayed amidst a rain of knives and torches thrown back and forth from all around her by three performers.

The woman's face and long black hair glittered with some sort of sparkly dust, and even more astounding was the music that she kept in perfect rhythm as it emmitted from the little bells in her bracelets and ankle-chains.

A band of musicians marched among the rabble. They intercepted Natir and Teyrnon's way and forced them to step aside.

The two of them stood on their toes with their backs to a

wall, waiting for the band to pass, with Natir bowled over by the bands' weird customs. Just then Natir noticed something that made her face shoot up, looking across the street with her jaw hung open.

There was a blonde locked inside a big bird's cage, hung in front of a store. The young woman was skin-bare to the world, save for white feathers glued to her breasts and groin. Her skin shined with oil, and she had wings attached to her shoulders.

The mere sight of her made Natir shiver from the cold. She couldn't comprehend the kind of tolerance the woman must have had not to cry for a dress before she might freeze to death, much less keep the smiles and siren looks she was throwing at the passersby as she crocked her finger for every man to come inside.

Natir failed to hear Teyrnon over the sound of the duffs and flutes, so he grabbed her upper arm and leaned close to her ear when she looked at him.

Raising his voice, he said, "Stay close. We're almost there."

She nodded and followed him.

*   *   *

"Teyrnon!" A mature woman arrayed in purple and scarlet dress yelped with joy when she saw them walk into her store.

The woman got off her seat and welcomed Teyrnon with a hug so intimate, it made their bodies look like they were meant to complete one another.

"Oh, Teyrnon, I can't believe my eyes."

"Irenka."

"You're so cruel, you know how lonely my heart has been without you?"

Natir, who was turning her face about, inspecting the place, soon had her attention stolen by Irenka's hands as they slowly glided over Teyrnon's back. Her eyes flung wide open as she stared at them.

Irenka's hands were painted with a work of art: a sad maiden emerging from the surface of a lake, gazing at the moon. On each of Irenka's fingers, she had a golden ring with pearls and precious stones, any one of them enough to buy Natir ten times over. As for the amount of engraved gems she had in her bracelets, it caused Natir's eyes to lose focus.

"Where have you been all this time?" Irenka murmured. "Come, you have to tell me everything."

"I'm actually—"

"Later. Come with me, come." Not wasting a moment, Irenka got a firm hold of Teyrnon's wrist and immediately attempted to snatch him to her.

'Den!' was the only word that flashed in Natir's mind; it was like witnessing a spider excited by her prey.

"Irenka, wait, wait!" He stopped her. "I can't."

"It's okay, it's not what you think," she lied through her teeth, "just come to the back for a moment, I want to show you something."

Teyrnon gently freed his wrist and held Irenka's palm in his hands. "You know I can't. Really."

Irenka smiled as she masterfully countered his rejection with an arm sliding smoother than a snake over his shoulder and around his neck as her silken body sank against him, allowing her face to rise slowly to one side of his head.

She whispered words of temptation into his ear whilst combing her fingers through the hair on the back of his head with one hand and tracing invisible lines over his chest with the other.

It was all too obvious what Irenka was after, and her long black hair failed to conceal her lips from Natir's eyes as she ended her invitation with a gentle bite on his earlobe.

"*Irenka.*"

"It will only be a moment."

"I'm sorry. I really can't." He broke their contact.

"You've got to be kidding me." She looked truly hurt by his rejection as she backed off a step, staring at his face with disbelief.

Irenka averted her face as she huffed and rubbed her temple. "This is ridiculous…" She looked at him again. "You know, the world is not exactly going to end if you let yourself enjoy a drink with a friend every once in a while."

Teyrnon waved his arms. Clearly, he was struggling to find something to say. "I'm sorry."

"Fine. Whatever. Curses, if every man who gets himself a companion acts the way you do, I'd be long out of business… So, what brings you back to me then? Obviously not because you *missed me.*"

Attempting to comfort her, he took a step in. "Irenka, you know that's not true."

Irenka stopped him with her palm to his chest before he

could embrace her shoulders and hissed as vicious as a disappointed woman can get, "I asked: *what is it?* Spill it."

Teyrnon faked a chuckle as he took a few steps back and put his arm over Natir. "Actually, we need your help with something, and I just know that no one can do it better."

She eyed Natir up and down with the hostility of a rival before a dubious expression painted her face. She sent her gaze back to Teyrnon. "That's not her. That's not Olfa. I heard she's a blonde."

"No." He chuckled. "Irenka, this is Natir. She's a friend of mine."

"Pleasure to meet you," Natir said.

"Oh, I see," she narrowed her gaze, pushed Teyrnon off of Natir with the tips of her fingers, separating them, and spun around Natir with no hurry, "so it's *just business* that brought you here? Just when I thought you couldn't make this any worse."

"What can I say? I'm truly sorry. But at least I got to see you again—"

"Save it." Irenka silenced him with a glare. "You'll need more than sweet words to fix this one." She resumed her inspection of Natir while mumbling quietly to herself, "*At least I got to see you again.* Hah! As if it was me who left in the first place."

She felt the rough fabric of Natir's clothes in her fingers then took Natir's hand and felt it before looking at one of the women in the store and offering her her hand.

"*Aaand* who exactly did you say this peasant is trying to impress? What's her target?" Irenka asked.

Natir's jaw dropped before the blatant insults while the woman Irenka had signaled wiped Irenka's hand clean.

"An earl," said Teyrnon.

"Just an earl? Now, that's a low bar." She looked at them when the woman was done. "You know, an earl is just a village chief with an attitude. She doesn't need to waste her money and my time over something like this."

"This earl is different."

"Rubbish."

He approached her. "He's different. Very different."

"Let's say he is. What's in it for you? What are you plotting?"

"You know me better than to ask that."

"Yes, but still—"

He took her hand in his palms and looked straight into her eyes.

"It's a long story," he said softly. "Just know that I'm only trying to help, but I can't do it without you… It's going to be a bit tricky, Irenka. She needs no less than the best of our help. I'm asking you to do me this favor."

She quickly silenced him with her forefinger to his lips and murmured, "*Hush… Say no more.*"

"Irenka?"

She gave in to her feelings and soothed his cheek with the palm of her hand like she was admiring a sculpture. "If it's a favor you want, you only need to ask once, *never a second time.* Cursed are the days that made you forget that promise of mine."

He took her little hand and kissed it. "How could I ever

forget?"

"What...exactly are we talking about again?" Natir interrupted the lovely couple before a fairy might spark to life from the looks in their eyes.

They looked at her, so Natir shrugged and shifted her gaze to the merchandise. "We're just here for a dress, aren't we?"

Irenka smiled sweetly and approached Natir.

She held Natir's face in her hands. "Well, the raw material looks fine. It's nothing that I can't work—"

She'd gone silent midsentence and grimaced once she removed Natir's cape.

One of the two other women present who worked for Irenka gasped with shock and covered her mouth whilst her friend hurried to the entrance and pulled the curtain down before someone might see Natir.

"*Short hair?*" Irenka hissed. She stared daggers at Teyrnon. "She's a slave."

"No, she's not. Not anymore."

One woman said, "You want to tarnish the reputation of this place?"

Her friend echoed, "What do you want people to think of us? We don't handle slaves here. Take her and leave, now."

"I said she's not a slave, all right?"

"And what exactly do you expect me to do with *this?*" Irenka snapped, holding a handful of Natir's hair. "Forget an earl, not even the stupidest commoner wouldn't know how low to price this."

"Price...what?" Natir asked.

"That's...that's why we need your help."

Irenka buried her face in her palms. "I can't believe you're doing this to me. Please tell me the one she's after knows about this, at least. Give me that much to work with."

"He does. He does."

"You can't be serious," a woman said with worry, but Irenka's glare silenced her.

Irenka then turned to Natir with such a serious look, it made Natir anxious. "Ladies," she clapped her hands, "show her the way. You know what to do, start from the very bottom."

The other two women hesitated and stared at one another.

Irenka hissed at them, "I said, *show her the way.*"

"Come this way."

"What...where to? Teyrnon?" Natir stammered and looked over her shoulder at Teyrnon as the women led her to the back.

"Go with them. Go."

"But—"

"Just go. Don't worry, I'll find out where Alfred will be at and then meet you at the tavern down the road when you're done. Got it? The tavern down the road."

Once Natir and her guides disappeared behind a door, Teyrnon pushed a couple of coins into Irenka's hand. "For your trouble."

Her eyes flung wide open, "What the...are you insulting me?"

He closed her hand over the coins and said softly, "*Never.*

But this kind of thing has its costs, and I wouldn't feel right letting you shoulder the whole burden alone," he held her chin in his hand, "and maybe when I return, we can catch up on lost time. Share that drink you offered and—"

She suddenly stood on her toes, threw her arms around him and surprised him with a searing kiss that left him breathless.

Gasping for breath and her ruby lips wet with the sweet remnants of their fleeting union, she whispered, "Let's leave it at that."

"I—"

"*Hush*," she murmured alluringly with her hands holding on to his shirt, "no more words. Just leave it at that. Leave what's after *and* to chance."

She then strolled towards the back of the store, shaking her hips and dropping the coins onto the floor as she went. "That would be your payment."

*   *   *

Irenka could not fake preeminence any longer. She had been weakened by emotion, so much so that once she passed through the door, she staggered and leaned her back against a wooden post to ease her weight off her shaking legs.

She set her palm to her chest, tilted her head back and stared at the ceiling with a dreamy look in her eyes and let out the warm breath she'd been holding in.

Smiling, Irenka stepped through the beaded curtain that separated the two small rooms and entered just as the women were removing Natir's clothes. She needed to take only one look at Natir's legs for her smile to vanish and her cheeks to glow red with anger.

"What, is, that?"

"What?" Natir turned her face, clueless, between Irenka and her own feet. "It's puttees… It's just stripes of wool you wrap on your—"

"I know what puttees are. What is it doing on your feet?"

"What do you mean? It's winter. The world is covered with snow."

Irenka shook her head. "Take it off."

"But my feet will get cold."

"Oh, really? My, I'm so, so sorry. Tell you what, let me rephrase what I said last…" She approached her and hissed in Natir's face, "Take it off, or I'll burn it where it is."

Natir swallowed and turned to one of the women. "Help me take it off, please?"

Chapter 3

BEAUTIFUL ART

"Earl Alfred!"

Bertwin, earl of the Ulaky, got off his seat to welcome Alfred with open arms when he saw him walk into the hospitality house with some of his men.

Alfred barely managed to hide his surprise at seeing how much his friend had changed in the years they had not see one another.

The earl he remembered was a fierce man, a tall, proud, and battle-hardened Boii who inspired awe in whatever land he treaded. But this bellied old man in his fifties with deep wrinkles around his eyes and gray locks taunting his long black hair and beard, limping in his walk and dressed in clothing that barely fit him, could not have been the cupbearer of his friend.

"Earl Bertwin."

Bertwin laughed and embraced Alfred. "Look at you! I swear, you haven't aged a day since I last saw you. How long has it been, eight, nine years?"

"I could have said the same about you if it wasn't for that belly of yours. The Ulaky women are feeding you well, I see."

He cracked a laugh. "That they do, that they do. Fedor,

FEDOR, come here."

Fedor, a young man with strong resemblance to Bertwin, approached them.

"You remember Fedor, my son."

"How can I not? You've grown to be the spitting image of your father," Alfred patted the young man's shoulder, "and you've even had your first beard! You're a true man now."

"Thank you, sir."

Bertwin humored, "I must warn you, Alfred, the word going around the women's bowers is that my good looks are not all this fellow has gotten from his old man. They're not setting their eyes on this one like thieves for nothing."

"Ah! Now I know for certain that this pup is the son of that old wolf." He humored, "But where are your brothers, Fritz and Val?"

Bertwin's face darkened with grief. "They didn't make it."

Alfred responded under his breath, "I'm sorry."

Bertwin headed back to his table, thwacking loudly against the wooden floor with his benumbed leg and calling strongly on his way, "And neither did any of my other nine sons and daughters. Morana has had her say, and she claimed her honoring *at every cursed winter*, and one by one she took them all. Fedor and his half-sister, Antigone, are the ones Veles blessed me with. They are all I have left. Now come, Earl Alfred, wait for no invitation to sit at my table and share my drink. You are earl now, after all."

* * *

The place was small, rich with warmth, and a total mess of maquillage and apparel thrown about wherever she looked.

At the center of this jumble, Natir stood bare and stiff as a log, feeling like meat in the hands of cooks as three women busily worked on her.

One of them was done drying Natir's body—after they had bathed her—but then returned with fragrances to adorn Natir with.

Another woman had a vexed look on her face as she tried to paint something nice on the little she had to work with of Natir's bitten nails.

The third, who didn't bother to hide her irritation from Natir, was neatening Natir's hair with unrestrained brutality that caused Natir's head to be thrown back, and the noise of her comb ripping hair from the scalp echoed within Natir's skull with every stroke.

It was painful, yet Natir didn't dare open her mouth and tell the woman to take it easy on her before she went bald. She was embarrassed enough as she was, as next to her lay the gorgeous craved wooden tub that was once filled with beautiful rose petals floating over the surface of dim-pink hot water, now turned ash-gray from the hard scrubbing they had given her in there.

The women didn't say anything as they washed the stubborn layer of dirt off Natir's skin, but the looks they gave her were enough to make Natir drop her face and blame no one but herself for not rubbing the wet rags harder in the rare and frigid moments of privacy she had in the wagon over the past few days.

Irenka went through Natir's clothes left on a table. "Trash… Trash… Trash." She then addressed a younger woman standing by, "These won't do. Go get her a real dress."

"The blue one from the other night?"

Irenka inspected Natir with her eyes and said with some pointing and hand signals, "No, something with a lighter color. The thighs, waist, and face, that's what she needs to focus on." She bobbed her head, signaling Natir. "You there, Natir. This earl of yours, is he left or right-handed?"

"What? Oh, um, right-handed."

Irenka instructed the younger woman, "The ivory dress, the one open to the left. I think it's on the lower shelf."

The woman hesitated and turned her face between Natir and Irenka. "She got a wound to her waist," she said quietly. "The skin is still raw. It will show with such a dress."

The frown she received from Irenka in return made her hurry to the other room. "I'll go get it."

Irenka huffed, turned back to the table, and threw Natir's clothes onto the floor one piece after another when something caught her eye and she picked it up.

"Very *nice*!"

She admired the wooden comb with flowers, a stream, and barn swallow with wings kissing the moon engraved on it.

"Where did you get this? I don't imagine it's something you can easily afford."

"It was a gift," Natir said. "A friend made it for me."

"Made it for you?" She raised a brow then inspected the comb more closely. "Now, why would a woman make something like this for another?"

Her face darted towards Irenka. "How did you know?"

"Well, it's obvious, isn't it? It's too delicate...the details...the teeth are very even and their tips are smoothened. And the river is flowing from the left. This isn't something a man's hands could make, much less choose such fascinating scenery. And yet you tell me that she's just a friend, not a relative?"

"Yes."

"A lover perhaps?"

The women chuckled, causing Natir to frown.

"Just a dear friend."

"Okay, okay, we believe you." Irenka suppressed a laugh then waved the comb in her hand and made her offer, "Would you care to sell it to me? I'll give you two denarius for it."

"Thank you, but it's the only one I have—*Aagh!*" She yelped from the pain of another stroke.

"Four denarius then, and you get to pick any two combs you like from the ones I have."

"Thank you, but I don't wish to sell. It's dear to me and— *Yaah!*"

It was clear by now the pain was deliberate. Natir threw a glare at the woman behind her, who feigned innocence.

"What a shame. I really like it," Irenka said, flipping the comb in her palm, then raised her voice, "Aenor!"

"Yes?" the young woman responded from the other room.

"Get me the ivory-and-yellow belt, too."

"Yes."

"Ada, you're done with the fingernails yet?" Irenka asked.

"It will dry in a moment. I'll do her waist next, it's almost ready."

"Keep it lax, nothing too fancy."

"Like I have time for fancy," Ada mumbled as she headed towards a corner of the room where her tools were.

The other women also took a step back, so Natir took the chance of her momentary freedom to inspect herself.

Natir was sure she had felt Ada run her brushes all over her waist and upper arm earlier, but now that Natir checked it out, there was nothing there! No painting, no colors, just the warm feeling of something gooey and transparent on her skin.

"Don't touch it!" Ada's yell caused Natir to freeze before she could lay hand on her waist. "I am *not* going to do it all over again. Keep your arm up. Don't mess with my work," she warned as she returned with a frown on her face and a pot at hand.

"Hold still," the other woman instructed. She too had returned with a ribbon and got a hold of Natir's hair.

Ada asked her friend, "Can you do it while she's laying down? I need to do this now."

"Yes, sure."

They made Natir lie down on her side, where one woman parted Natir's hair to section out the strand above her ear —the only strand long enough to reach Natir's shoulder, which Cahal had allowed her to keep when he severed her hair. The woman then masterfully divided it in her hands into five parts and braided the middle three together all the way to the end like tight lace.

She then looped one end of the ribbon around her other hand's thumb, set it in Natir's hair, and weaved the tight braid she had made along with the other two sections loosely around it.

The interlock of dissimilar braids and adoring ivory ribbon, all beautifully blended into one, was fascinating, like a gentle waterfall that made Natir's hair look much thicker than it was.

As her hair was still being worked on, Natir curiously peeked down at what the other woman, Ada, was doing.

Ada had unveiled the golden dust she had in her pot, which she poured on Natir's waist and upper arm before she picked one of her brushes and carefully dusted it off.

To Natir's surprise, the dust adhered to the gooey material and revealed the painting Ada had drawn on her earlier. Natural patterns captured the candles' light and glittered like gold on Natir's skin, almost entirely concealing her wound.

The lines Ada had created—seemingly gentle, few, and loose at the bottom—branched off and interwoven violently together the further they went up like sparks shooting out of a bonfire until they created a seemingly impenetrable canopy in the form of two magnificent roses arrayed by leaves and twisted vines.

The look of bewilderment Natir had in her eyes turned to astonishment by the women's work. She had not seen such elegance since she first met Diva in Alfred's house, with the striking beauty of Diva's makeup and barn-swallow tattoo.

Ada then ran her brush here and there, scattering just a pinch of the golden particles on Natir's body at random.

"Breuci art," Irenka explained to her astonished client. "It's very popular in Wenclas in nowadays."

"Yes, but...that's gold!"

The women laughed.

"Well, you're not entirely wrong," Irenka said. "Many elites will accept nothing less than real gold dust. But this is just fool's gold—Pyr. It's practically worthless."

"Oh!" Natir sighed with relief, glad that she wasn't wasting something so expensive on herself, and whom have the women been expecting to pay for it? At the same time, she was also slightly disappointed.

"Beautiful, isn't it?" Irenka resumed. "Ada excels in the arts of her people, she might very well be the best in Wenclas, and her services are not cheap."

"Thank you," Natir said.

In response, Ada meanly sent her brush at Natir's face, causing her to turn trying not to sneeze.

"It's not meant for slaves."

"Ada!" Irenka warned.

"Just a finishing touch." She shrugged innocently then threw Natir a narrow gaze. "Morana knows that slave-face needs it."

As Ada returned her tools, Natir sat up on her elbow and checked her braid, then the golden paint, which she hesitated to touch.

"How do you remove it?"

Ada froze in her tracks. Her eyes flung wide open. She turned her face to Natir and hissed, "*Excuse me?* Are you trying to tell me something?"

"What? No, no, that's not what I meant. It's really beautiful, and, um, I was just asking, won't it come off if I touch it?"

Ada shook her head and continued her way while Irenka answered for her.

"It won't. The excess dust will sprinkle at start, but don't you worry, in a little bit the mixture will fully dry and maintain its shape even if you rub it or get it wet. It will last a fortnight, easy. But if you're asking how to remove it on purpose, then there are two ways to do that. One: use a mixture of water, salt, and vinegar."

Rubbing salt and vinegar over her freshly healed skin didn't sound that tempting. "And the other way?"

"Rip your own skin off."

Natir opted to use salt and vinegar.

Aenor returned to the room and offered Irenka the woven belt. "This one?"

"Yes. Now, help her with the dress."

They dressed Natir with a white, soft scarf that they wrapped elegantly around her hips for loincloth.

Natir admired the final result. The scarf wasn't just tied around her hips as Natir would have normally done but braided linearly to one side with its three extensions, one longer than the other two, left hanging loosely by her side.

The wrapping style was so attractive, it made Natir worry. There was no way she could hope to replicate the women's work by herself once the scarf was undone, and it really looked as though it was meant to be worn alone, for a night of passion.

Natir stopped Aenor before she could put the dress over her head. "Wait, what about my chest?"

Aenor chuckled. "You don't wear anything like that underneath such dress, *silly*. Now, put your arms up."

The dress they helped her into was just as thin as the scarf. Natir felt sure that her nipples would show.

Concerned, Natir asked, "You know, it's really cold outside, can I at least—" She went silent midsentence when she saw Irenka messing with her comb. "What are you doing?"

Irenka had used the woven belt's straps to tie the comb to the belt. She then approached Natir and wrapped the belt around her waist.

"You were saying?"

Natir looked down at her comb, dandling to her side. "But it's a comb, not an accessory."

She tapped Natir's forehead. "Everything is an accessory meant to attract attention. Your dress, your comb, your hips, your breasts, your eyes, and your hair. A woman's body is a glory of attractions *if* she wishes to use it in such way. So, what do you think?"

Natir inspected her looks. "It's...all lovely. But is all of this really necessary?"

Irenka narrowed her gaze. "What's *necessary* is something I can't give you overnight," she said. "I'll be honest with you, Natir. I don't share Teyrnon's optimism. As you are now, snagging a man for yourself is a bet I wouldn't put my money on. But we were able to mend your looks at least. You'll have to make do with that much and maybe good luck will have its say."

It felt like a blow to her ego. Natir frowned. "I know how to snag a man's attention."

"Do you?" She suppressed a laugh. "All right then, I believe we got time for this. So, go ahead and show us."

"Show what?"

Irenka shrugged. "Show us. Pretend we're men and seduce us."

"Well, um—"

"What's the problem?" she asked, causing the women to chuckle.

"Maybe the scene is not convincing." Ada laughed.

"All right then, I'll make it easier for you," Irenka said. "I'm going to stand right here. I want you to pretend that I'm the earl you wish to bring to his knees and show me how you're going to charm me from the first step you take through that door."

"You're serious?"

"Does it look like I'm joking…? Well, what's the matter? It shouldn't be much to ask from a real woman to earn herself a single gaze of affection, is it? And I'm sure we all have *much* to learn from the secrets of seduction of the women of your people."

The women covered their mouths, chuckling.

Natir snapped, "Fine!" She barged out of the room.

The women whispered with joy, "You're so mean."

"She's really going to do it."

Irenka signaled them to keep quiet.

Natir walked back inside, smiling and waving her hand at Irenka, but it only caused the women to laugh at her while Irenka pretended to rub her temple to hide her smile.

Natir raised her voice, feeling embarrassed, "Well, of course it's not going to work like this. We're all women and...and you were expecting it. You didn't even give me the chance to say something!"

"Ladies, please," Irenka silenced them. "Ada, will you please repeat what Natir just did?"

"What? Why me?"

"Just do it, please."

Ada mumbled as she went behind the door's curtain, "I'll have to put on a damn good act to look that bad."

Repeating Natir's show, the women burst out with insane laughter at Ada.

"Oh, go fuck yourselves!" Ada yelled.

"Aenor," Irenka called, fighting back laughter, "it's your turn now. Will you please show us how *a woman* enters?"

"Yes!" Aenor yelped excitedly and rushed out of the room.

Then, with one foot leading the other, Aenor cat-walked back inside like she owned the place. She entered the scene like a song with every step she took playing a tune and her very body a melody.

One woman laughed while the others clapped their hands or called out with cheers at her performance, prompting Aenor to make a comical bow.

"You see the difference, Natir?"

"That doesn't—"

"The best woman makes the best thief," Irenka lectured as she circled slowly around Natir. "Stealing a man's attention is exactly what it sounds like: *a steal*. Either you do it in a flash or not at all. You complained that you didn't have a chance to say something? You didn't get to *charm him* with your words? Oh, *puh-lease*! Save that excuse for the losers, for by the time you open your mouth, the next woman that walks through that door would have already stolen your man's eyes, and now he belongs to her."

Natir was startled to her toes when Irenka suddenly embraced her from behind, her arms feeling Natir's body the way a man would to a woman.

"You're a *woman*," she whispered, "so be a woman. Greet your man with your body before your lips and leave the words for when the candles are no longer lit."

Irenka then approached Aenor. She stood behind her and surrounded Aenor's shoulders with her arm.

"Aenor here is my newest apprentice," she said, "and an *excellent thief*. Aenor, love, why don't you show our guest some of the tricks you've learned? Start with the basics. Little girls' things."

Chapter 4

CHANGE OF PLANS

Alfred had been keeping to himself until he saw where this thing was going, but his friend's odd behavior—trying a bit too hard to turn their reunion to an event worth celebrating—had been gnawing at him for a while.

"So, the Toic and Ulaky are fighting together again!" Bertwin cheered and raised his drink. A young woman sat on his lap, and between himself and Alfred, all the seats on the table were occupied by their men.

Alfred responded with a fake smile, "So it seems."

"This calls for a better drink than this. Veles knows I hate the soft taste." He turned to a man who stood behind him. "Well, what are you waiting for, you dumb stick—?"

"Bertwin." Alfred tried to interrupt, but his friend wasn't listening.

"Go find us some real southern wine to drink and a postpartum maid with a fine face to hold my jug between her swollen breasts."

The man looked perplexed. He exchanged an awkward look with one of his friends. Even the woman seated on Bertwin's lap had to suck on her lower lip not to laugh.

"Did you not hear me?" Bertwin threw the cup at the man.

"Yes, sir." He nudged one of his friends to help him carry

out their earl's odd demand.

Alfred couldn't help but chuckle. "Postpartum?"

"The sight of a woman's wet nipples staining her shirt excites me. And don't you dare tell me you don't feel the same."

Alfred shook his head, laughing, then motioned at Bertwin's leg and asked, "What happened to your leg?"

"Ah, you mean this? The cold must have gotten to me on my way here. I woke up two days ago and it was numb as a rock, but it's nothing that a good night's sleep can't fix. Don't worry about it."

Alfred's face grew hard. He stared ahead at Bertwin. His friend's eluding answers and how he was clearly pushing himself beyond his limit were the last straw.

"Bertwin," Alfred set down his cup, "what are you doing here?"

"What…? What kind of a question is that?"

"The Ulaky are not obliged to aid Valdes. You don't need to be here, this is not your war."

Bertwin's expression changed to one of chagrin. He tiredly led the woman off his lap. "Go now, my dear. I'll tip you later," he told her then turned to Fedor and the rest. "All of you, go. Leave us alone for a while."

Alfred motioned his men to leave the table as well, and they resumed their conversation once it was just the two of them.

"Alfred, you are like family to me, and one of very few men whom I trust with my secrets."

"And I do value your trust." Alfred drank then commented,

"I've heard you had some trouble up north."

"Ah! You mean the Arochy? It was nothing."

"You could have called for my aid at any time, but you didn't."

"It wasn't worth it, the whole thing was a joke. The bastards grew bold and decided to poke my side once or twice to see if I'm dead or napping, and I've beaten them back each time."

"What's the problem, then?"

Bertwin leaned forward. "I'm getting old, my friend. I have outlived the years of my father, and time has wilted me."

"You woke up with a numb leg, and it made you pity yourself to death? This is not the Bertwin that I know."

"You are not listening. I'm getting much too old for this business of ours. I'm old. The Ulaky are old. And the poor years of sickness and dearth have gotten the best of us... These past few skirmishes I had have opened my eyes, Alfred. I am not the man I used to be."

Alfred pushed his drink over to Bertwin, who took it in both hands.

"They are young and prospering," Bertwin resumed, speaking with bitterness.

"The Arochy?"

"And many others. Many. And they want what all young want from the world: more of everything. The poets sing of my triumphs over them. They call my enemies fools who can't hope to grasp the wind of me. But in truth, I'm the one who can barely keep up with them. You should have seen them, Alfred. They fell like true men should and died a death you can only wish for yourself… *Heroes.* Hah! There was a time when I yearned to find one to kill. Nowadays, it seems as if every clan has a hero of their own. But what do the Ulaky have? A name? Honor? Ancient glory? What are these things worth when the blades are drawn?"

"If you're worried they might try something again, you can always count on the Toic's—"

"That's not what I need!"

Alfred was taken aback by his friend's outburst.

Bertwin resumed more calmly, "Yes, I know the old alliances still hold. I know I have a friend or two I can rely on. But for *how long*…? What I really need, my friend, is *time*. Time for my son to stand on his own feet. Time for the Ulaky to indemnify what they've lost and stand strong again. That is why I am here. This unexpected campaign is exactly the kind of elixir of life I need to secure the survival of my people."

"You're hoping for Valdes's favor?"

"I'm hoping for his gold."

"Ah!"

"Valdes is on the move and the Teranians have got his back. Ardent has no clue whom he's messing with, they will trample over him like dirt. So, you see, this war is the safe bet I've been waiting for to get the gold and slaves I need to extend our existence long enough for my son and the Ulaky to pull themselves together. That is why I've bet everything I have on this."

Alfred averted his gaze and nodded then asked, "How

many?"

"Seven hundred."

The number took Alfred by surprise. "I didn't realize the Ulaky could muster so many men."

"We can't," he said with a sly look, "not with *reason*."

Alfred turned his face about, looking uncomfortable. "New blood? They've never seen a battle before?"

"And peasants who never held a weapon before."

"You're just maximizing your numbers and hoping for a bigger share? Have you thought what will happen when they see a real fight?"

"There will be no fight," said Bertwin. "They probably won't even see a single sword drawn in their faces. Between Valdes and the Teranians, Ardent and his allies will break in a day, and the rest is just spoils for the taking."

"That's a very risky game you're playing."

"It's a risk I have to take, and the gods have already proved my decision right. You can see what I mean, can't you? This reunion is a blessing for us both. I've brought more men than most others, and you hold Valdes's favor and trust. He considers you more than an ally, he sees you as a friend. So, imagine when the Ulaky and Toic arrive to his aid together? Between his trust in you and my numbers, we are certain to rise above the others and secure a decent share of the spoils."

The latter part was news to Alfred. He leaned forward and asked, "Arrive to his aid?"

"Yes," Bertwin said, his excitement causing him to miss

Alfred's point, "that is why we need to be swift on our feet. We must move out first thing in the morning and join up with him before too long. We can't afford to be the last to arrive."

Alfred asked again, "Valdes has already left Wenclas?"

"You didn't know?"

"I was told he was going to set camp here, refurbish his troops, and wait to join forces with the rest of us."

"That's what I thought as well. If I had known he's in such a hurry to face Ardent, I would not have wasted any time getting here. But by the time I did, he had already gone ahead. Then I had to waste a day for my men to get some rest, but that's all I can afford to give them."

Alfred frowned. He turned to where his men had gathered and called, "Ernust!"

His man approached them, and Alfred instructed him, "Find Earhart and Agatha and tell them to make sure the men stay with the wagons and horses and not to wander off. I want every man accounted for."

"Yes."

"Also, tell them that we're not staying as planned and will depart first thing in the morning."

Bertwin relaxed back against his seat. "I'm glad to hear we're of the same mind."

"Old friend, I'm sorry to tell you this, but we're not."

"What?"

Alfred leaned forward and whispered, "Bertwin, you've

shared your thoughts with me. Now, allow me to return the courtesy and share mine: I plan on talking Valdes out of this."

Bertwin needed a moment to find his voice. "What nonsense are you talking about?"

Chapter 5

WHERE THE PEARL SLEEPS

"Let's get you a sandal that goes with that dress," Irenka said as she led Natir by her hand to her own bedroom, "but first…"

Irenka took a moment to pick a hair extension braid from over a dozen she had lined on the wall, while Natir turned about admiring the luxury that surrounded her and all the valuables and personal treasures Irenka had in there.

A dark-brown wooden holder caught Natir's eye. On top of it lay over a dozen engraved wooden combs, each of them a rival for the one Diva had gifted her. They even had matching handheld mirrors with an identical engraving.

Next to it was a seemingly endless number of expensive silky scarfs piled up in a colorful jumble or thrown carelessly under the roamers' feet; dresses and sandals, the likes of which Natir could never afford, filled the shelves on the wall and two large boxes on the floor. There was even a small box loaded with earrings and necklaces left wide open on a nearby stand.

"Turn around."

Natir spun on her heel and saw that Irenka had returned with the braid she had picked.

She positioned Natir, back towards her, and dressed the

braid to the back of Natir's head. Irenka then ran her fingers through Natir's hair with a lot of care, brushing it until she was satisfied the braid merged perfectly.

"Much better."

Natir was about to reach out to inspect the braid, but Irenka stole her hand and led her to a full-length wooden frame with a thin polished sheet of silver on its surface. She stood behind Natir, her palms on Natir's shoulders and her lips a tender smile as they gazed onto the mirror together.

Softly, she whispered in her ear, "Now, you're a woman again."

Natir was at a loss for words as she examined her reflection.

Her heart throbbed out of control as she held the braid in her trembling hands and silently gaped at it. The thick, silky brown hair with gleams of warm lights was a perfect match to hers, and it felt exactly as if it were her own hair she was feeling in her fingers once again.

Her hands moved not by will but by emotions alone as her palms tenderly closed together over the braid and brought it close to her face where she shut her eyes and sniffed the faint bewitching scent.

Natir could not believe it. No woman could possibly mistake something like this. It even smelled the same. Exactly the same. The wonderful feeling caused her mind to go numb, like embracing a long-faded memory so beautiful, it could make her cry.

Tears almost sprang to her eyes.

"Why are you doing this?" she asked, breathless with

emotion. "I know it's not because Teyrnon paid you."

"Paid me?" Irenka snickered. "Love, if I were to charge Teyrnon the same as other men, he wouldn't afford my smile. This braid in your hands alone is worth twenty times over what he thought he paid for."

"Then why?" Her own voice was alien to her, so ravaged by her emotions that it became but a breeze tottering blossoms.

Irenka motioned towards the shoes' shelves. "Go. Pick a sandal." She headed in the opposite direction to a small box she had on a table. "Consider a pair of nude shoes, it will be a good choice that extends the line of your legs. And no puttees this time! I don't care how cold you think it is, a woman's ankles are not meant to be covered."

Natir chose a sandal and seated herself on the bed's edge. She asserted again as she slipped it on, "You still didn't answer me."

"I was just about to, and it might as well count as another lesson for you…"

Her back to Natir, Natir could not see what it was that Irenka held in her hands, just silently staring at it.

Irenka released a warm breath and shut her eyes as she brought her hands to her chest. She placed whatever she was holding back into the box and turned around, facing Natir, and rested her lower back against the table.

"Years ago," she started, "when I first arrived at this place, I did the stupidest thing: I went for easy money the same way most women who come here do. It paid well, of that you can be sure. And yet somehow, I was always broke! I just didn't understand what it was that I was doing wrong, so much so that I couldn't afford a single night's rest."

"It's that expensive to live here?"

"Very. Well, among other things, I wasted my money. But that wasn't the real problem. You see, I was stuck entertaining the strapped dregs of this town and almost never had the same bastard ask for me twice. And those who did, it was only because they didn't remember they had me before."

Natir's eyes flung open. "You're joking."

She shrugged. "Just imagine what something like that can do to a woman's ego. All the while, jealousy burnt my heart for all the stories I kept hearing of women earning in one night what I didn't dream to make in a lifetime. I tried everything I could think of to turn my luck around. Dresses, maquillage, cheap acts and foolish adventures, you name it, but it was all for nothing. It...it was driving me mad! Just what was it that those women had that I didn't...? Then, one rainy night, I was picked up by a *younger man*. The pay he offered wasn't great, but anything is better than standing in the rain waiting for nothing, right? And at least he was feasible to my eyes."

"Was it—"

Irenka raised her palm, stopping Natir before she could finish.

"Just hold on," Irenka said. "This is where the story gets interesting... Then, just as I lay with him and was about to peel my wet clothes off, the young man said," a chuckle escaped through her nose. Irenka averted her face, smiling with embarrassment, "Well…he said something odd."

Irenka's smile proved contagious. Natir had to ask, "What did he say?"

"He said, out of the blue: I heard of an amazing blue sea, far, far away, where pearls roll and play all day long with unmatched happiness."

"What?" Natir asked and snickered together, not making any sense of that line at all.

"I know, right? That's exactly how I felt. And all I could respond with was raising an eyebrow at him and saying: *Okay*…! And I thought to myself that he must be nervous, and I better take it easy on him."

"Yes, exactly."

"But then, imagine this, he made it even more awkward. He just went on talking and said: All of them were happy, every last pearl of them was filled with joy, because they were home, and loved, and cared for. *Except for one pearl…* You see, the poor little pearl was different from all the rest. Other pearls were white, ivory and pink, but she was the only one as black as the night. She always stood out among them and could not get along with the other pearls. So, one day, the little pearl decided to find herself a home. A place where she truly belongs, so that she too can be happy like all pearls should—

"So, she set out on a journey that she could not foresee how it would end and asked the stingray: Stingray, do you know where my home is? And the stingray told her that he didn't know and that she should ask the Pilcard, for that they travel more and have seen more places. So, she asked the Pilcard next: Pilcards, do you know where my home is? And the Pilcard told her that they didn't know, either, and that she will have better luck asking the octopus, for that he is wiser—

"And the young man went on and on, naming sea creatures that I've never ever heard of, and the whole time I was just staring at him, thinking: *what is this man talking about?*"

Natir burst out with a laugh. "Was he drunk?" she asked.

"Better. He was the passionate type," she said and bit her lower lip.

"So, finally," Irenka resumed, "our little pearl came ashore and asked a wise young man: Young man, do you know where my home is? And the young man answered: Yes. I know where your home is. And I will take you there. And so, he took the poor pearl with him on an even longer journey across vast plains, high hills, and snowy mountains in an adventure filled with wonders and people and places the likes of which she had never imagined."

Irenka reached into the box, and right before Natir's bemused eyes, she dressed her neck with a leather necklace. Strapped at its end was a perfect *black pearl* resting at the very edge of her marvelous cleavage.

Her eyes to the pearl, Natir was stunned speechless. The fairytale had suddenly turned real! She met Irenka's gaze with lost eyes, eager for explanation.

Her smile was a tale of love. "And on the warm, soft chest of *the most beautiful woman the young man had ever seen*, he placed the little pearl and told her: *This is home*. And the little pearl's journey finally came to an end. She had found her loving home, her one true friend, and her happiness… Do I need to add that I was no longer in a hurry to finish him off that night?" She finished with a naughty wink.

The pearl was all that Natir could see anymore as she was left breathless in a moment of astonishment and envy.

Natir regained herself and smirked. "That young man was Teyrnon."

It sounded like him all right, only the tale he told Irenka was much nicer than the ones she had heard…and it came with an expensive gift.

"I was his first," she said with a hint of womanly pride in her voice, "and like any young man about to experience a woman's love for the first time, he was very nervous. Hence the gift that outweighed what he could afford."

"Quite the relationship you two have."

"You've learned but a drop in a bucket of it. That night changed everything for me. You see, he wasn't the handsomest, the richest, the strongest, or even the best sex I ever had. We're not even a match, and I can hope for no future with him. And yet, there I was, turning down real offers night after night and keeping my eye on the road eager to see him come my way again like a woman in love, not caring for a moment if he could afford me or not—

"I valued him that much. I valued his company more than anything, and I could never take what had happened between us out of my mind. And *that* opened my eyes to something that I don't know how I could have been so blind not to see it my whole life! It made me realize that I didn't need to be the prettiest, the sweetest, or even friends with someone important in order to stand out among other women. I just needed a story."

"Story? What story?"

"A story to be remembered by. No man will remember how warm it was inside of me. No one will tell his friends what my hair was combed like, the color of my eyes, and the things we did under the sheets. All of that means nothing. But, every time one of them sees a pearl, they will remember my story, they will share it with their friends, and my name will shine."

"I...don't think—"

"Think what you want, Natir," she said firmly. "Laugh even, if you so wish. But mark my words. Long after you forget what my face looks like, you will remember my pearl. Just like they all do."

"So, you've been telling men the story of your pearl ever since?"

She laughed. "Well, yes and no. It was spontaneous in the beginning, you know? I was simply that excited about it and told everybody, and before I knew it, they were all calling me *'the woman with the pearl'*. I had men with real money in their pouches come down my street looking to spend a night with *'the woman with the pearl'*. You should have seen it, it was ridiculous! After that, the rest was all too easy, and I started telling stories of my own. True or false, it didn't matter, so long as it resounded. I'd make up a story about my dress to one man, open up about my oldest childhood memory to another, and fabricate a fantasy about the earring I wore on one ear and how

I had found it at the bottom of my drink."

She approached Natir and sat next to her.

"The poorest of all women will have nothing to sell but her body, Natir," she said. "She will earn but her bread, and no one will remember her in an hour.. A smart woman will need to sell but snippets of attraction for more and will be remembered for much longer.. But a wise woman? A wise woman will steal her man's eyes with her looks, drain his might into her flesh, and when he lies there strengthless on her bed and all under her mercy, that's when she will bewitch his mind with her stories, claim his everything, and for as long as a lifetime shall last, so shall she be remembered. That's the power of storytelling."

She gently turned Natir's face towards her.

"You understand the lesson I'm trying to teach you, my love...?" she said softly and held Natir's hand in hers. "I have mentored the best seductresses this town has ever seen and brought down lords from their high seats, kissing my feet. You really think that a woman like me can't teach you how to bring that earl of yours to his knees, crying tears of passion for you...? The only question left, Natir, is what story will those lips whisper to your man, and what pearl sleeps at your chest?"

Chapter 6

CARNIVAL OF THE ROTTEN I

She walked out the door tall and lively, exactly as Irenka would have expected from a good student, but it was all an act propelled by her desire to escape another lecture, for once Natir was out of Irenka's sight, she curled in on herself and rubbed at the gooseflesh on her upper arms without a shred of feminine elegance.

Natir turned her head about, twittering from the cold in her light dress, and decided she better hurry up and meet with Teyrnon before the water of her mouth froze solid.

She made her way down the busy street, substantially slowed down by all the distractions in her path.

Everything was new and strange to her eyes, and the people were very different. They were arrogant, loud, and overfed, and the most detestable things were the norm in their lives.

Her gaze was snatched left and right by couples mating in plain sight and behind unveiled windows, young lovers, drunk friends, men with men, women with women, grey-haired with nippers, and the streetwalkers calling the men to their skirts who outnumbered the doors of town. No one else thought it bizarre. No desire was restricted, and the drunks were getting arrested by the dozens every night.

Suddenly, something startled Natir and brought her to an immediate stop. She gazed up with momentous awe, unsure what to do.

There was a band of performers coming her way, an army of giants in her eyes as they marched on nine-foot-long sticks concealed by their lengthened pants, playing their music and throwing burning sticks among themselves.

In her nervousness, she looked left and right then moved aside in a hurry to make way for them, while everyone else was hardly concerned by it and continued on, the band marching overhead.

Natir followed the performers with her eyes for a few moments, and when she turned to continue her way, her gaze fell on a small gathering of six or eight men directly ahead of her who were being exceptionally loud and joyful.

She stole one step after another, slowly moving closer and trying to figure out what they were laughing about, until she was standing a few steps from them.

The men were surrounding a friend of theirs who sat alone at a table waiting for something. He was well dressed, and his table had nothing but an abnormally long and thin spoon.

A fat woman stepped out of the shop.

She wore a black fluffy dress with no sleeves and great feathers attached to its back like a tail. A red star adorned her left eye, and her enormous breasts bounced as she walked.

The woman laughed with the rest as she set a covered pot in front of the man, then with a swift motion of her arms, she snatched the lid from over the pot and whatever was inside immediately burst into raging flames more intense than oil set on fire. It almost burned the man's face off.

Natir's face paled with worry. She could not tear her eyes off the scene, and the only thing on her mind was if that man was really going to eat from the pot.

The woman waved her arm, inviting the customer to begin. He cracked a wild laugh, dipped the spoon into the flame, and saluted the woman with it, accepting the challenge, and ate fire.

Natir's hand flew to her mouth in shock.

His friends' cheers and laughter went wild, and the man laughed with them until he realized the source of their amusement: his beard had caught fire! He panicked and fell to the floor, clapping at his beard.

The fat woman stopped laughing when she noticed Natir staring at them. With a devious look in her eyes, the woman set both her hands at her lips to blow Natir a kiss, and a sudden burst of fire shot out of her mouth four feet through the air towards Natir.

Natir shirked and leapt backwards, almost falling over herself.

She didn't wait a moment longer and rushed out of there, stealing looks over her shoulder at the woman who was still laughing at her and not knowing what to think of her sorcery.

After she had put ample distance between herself and the woman, Natir had just begun to catch her breath when a young man passing her made a sudden turnaround and walked next to Natir.

He matched her pace and made a filthy compliment about her legs that sent a shudder of shock and disgust through her skin.

A snort escaped Natir, and she threw him a look as she

walked but ultimately decided to ignore him. She strode faster, not dignifying his interest with a word, but he followed her and called out several times, asking Natir what her price was.

She shook her head in disbelief then glanced over her shoulder to see if the young man was still following her. Her distraction caused Natir to miss seeing the two men running in the opposite direction.

She yelped in surprise as she noticed them just in the nick of time and jumped out of the way before they could bump into her.

Two of the town's guards pursued close behind them. They tackled one of the men and beat him on the street with their sticks right under her sight. Natir watched with dismay as one guard repeatedly rammed the man's face onto the pavement until his teeth scattered about.

"Out of the way, out of the way!"

The cry startled her.

Another guard riding a horse had rushed to join his friends. After more cursing and beating, they tied the whimpering man's arms behind his back and his feet to the horse and dragged him away like the corpse of a boar.

It wasn't just the brutality of what had happened that shocked Natir but how everyone else carried along as usual throughout the whole thing. The laughter, the businesses, the women's wild yelps, and the music never stopped, and hardly anyone else bothered to watch.

She forced her legs to move and carried on her way,

determined not to get distracted again and waste time.

The tavern was just a short walk ahead now.

Natir was almost there—she could already recognize the distinguishable signs Irenka described for her—but yet again she found herself slowing down against her will.

Before she knew it, Natir had come to a complete halt. She was rapt by the sight of a woman who lay bare on a stone slab, twisting her body in every way amidst an audience.

Natir didn't quite get what was going on to stimulate the giggles and interest of so many onlookers. If anything, the woman's motion and moans made Natir think she was in fever.

"Excuse me." Overwhelmed by curiosity, she squeezed herself through the crowd to have a better look.

Moments later, Natir froze, stunned with her eyes flung wide open as she witnessed an eight-foot snake crawling all over the woman's body.

She stumbled backwards, her expression petrified with shock and her hands covering her gaping mouth, then made her escape. The woman was making love in public, to a snake!

Natir shook her head and mumbled to herself to hurry out of these streets of lunacy when, out of nowhere, a man's voice resounded.

"Just who I was looking for!"

The complete stranger, an elderly man overdressed with fancy garments, wrapped his arm around hers and snatched Natir, leading her in the opposite direction.

"Ah, excuse me!" Overtaken by awkwardness, Natir

attempted to free her arm without resorting to force.

"Is it destiny? Is it chance? Or is it just your lucky night that a man as magnificent as myself has noticed the spark of passion in your eyes tonight?" he said, loud and proud, strutting like a peacock.

"What...sir, sir, what are you doing? Will you please let go of my arm?" she said, stealing looks over her shoulder at the tavern as she was led farther and farther away.

"Well, call it what you wish or leave it a mystery, it doesn't matter. All that matters is that it finally happened, and now your future will be bright, bright, and *brriiight!*"

"Excuse me? Sir? Sir, will you please stop?"

He stopped and met her gaze at last but didn't let go of her just yet. "Yes, my dear. For you, I will spare a moment. What is it that you wish to buy? Just point it out to me and I shall—"

"I think you're mistaking me for someone else. I don't know you."

He cracked a laugh and resumed his way, pulling Natir with him. "Why, of course, you must be new here. How exciting. Truly exciting. Well, allow me to educate you, little flare. My name is Ukrit! I'm very famous, just mention my name to anybody and see how they'll humble themselves and bow their heads with respect..."

As the strange man dragged Natir onto a different street, another man who was secretly watching them from an alley pulled a scarf to conceal his face and prepared a dagger in his sleeve.

He had taken advantage of Ukrit's distraction and pushed himself out of the alley, hurrying after them.

"…and twenty-five horses and two hundred bulls," Ukrit bragged about his fortune to Natir, "and that was from two years ago! In my eastern estate alone! I've lost count ever since. I swear, my people would have long starved to death if it wasn't for the head on my shoulders."

"Look, that's good for you and all, but—"

"Seven times they begged me to become their earl, and seven times I refused."

"Will you please just listen? Look, sir, I really need to go. I've got someone waiting for me."

"Nonsense. Whatever he promised you, I'll triple—*Aghh!*"

It happened in a flash.

Suddenly, the man in disguise appeared behind Ukrit and stabbed him to the side of his chest, straight to the heart.

Before Natir could realize what had happened, the killer swiftly snatched her, pulled her by the wrist into himself, threw his arm around her, and led her forward, continuing their way as if nothing had happened.

"Uh…wait…what?" she stammered, trying to look back.

"Stay quiet," he whispered.

Just then, Natir felt his blade against her side.

"Keep walking. Act normal."

It took Natir a moment for the reality of what just happened to sink in. A cold wave ran through her body and sealed her lips tight as she instinctively complied to his commands.

She tried to steal looks back at the assassinated man and expected a ruckus to erupt, but all she caught were glimpses of a random person who hurried out to search Ukrit, stole his pouch, and took off with it. The blind had more sight in their eyes than anyone else who walked down that street.

The man stole Natir into a narrow alley, where he suddenly pushed her against a wall and put a quinar—silver coin—in her hand.

"For your kiss of silence."

"For my what?"

Before the words were fully out of her mouth, he had forced himself on Natir, kissing her, then disappeared into the dark of the alley as swift as he had appeared.

Natir froze in place for several moments, panting for air and feeling her knees tremble with shock as she relived the entire scene in her head, realizing she could so easily be dead by now at this very spot without anyone batting an eye or even noticing it.

White breaths racing on her violated lips, she looked down at the coin in her trembling hand then stole a look around the building at the dead body in the middle of the street.

Natir told herself that she couldn't stay where she was for long.

She hid the coin in her dress, slapped her palms to her face and sucked in deep breaths to calm her nerves before she walked back onto the street, retracing her steps and rushing by the dead body without looking at it.

* * *

"You tell me you are up in arms with the swords of the Toic at your back *to stop the war*?" Bertwin asked, angry but managing to keep his voice down.

"That's exactly what I'm telling you," said Alfred.

"Have you gone mad? Didn't I just tell you how important this campaign is for me? You know how many others feel the same? If you came out talking rubbish like that—"

"But I'm not coming out with it." Alfred eyed him back. "Not even to my own men. I'm only sharing this with you, as a friend."

"Alfred?"

"This is Morana's domain," he said firmly. "The Boii have not fought under her sight in a hundred years and for a very good reason: A campaign in winter can only end up in calamity for both sides. What Valdes and Ardent are doing is unthinkable… Now, I have good relationship with both of them, and I plan to exploit that relationship to meddle in their affairs and negotiate a truce before it's too late."

"It's you who's speaking the unthinkable." Bertwin grabbed his arm and leaned toward him to whisper, "If a word of this comes out, you may not even make it to Valdes before a dagger finds your back. Maybe even by one of my own men."

"Are you threatening me?"

"I am counseling you. Take that stupid idea out of your head and swim with the flow. We need to work together, you and I, we have a great opportunity here—"

"Father?"

Not a child, not yet a woman. The thirteen-year-old interrupted them. She had a slender build that was perfect for her age and long, braided black hair. Her cheeks were flushed, and she had kindness in her deep brown eyes.

The two men set the tensed atmosphere aside, each on his own.

"Oh, Antigone." Bertwin pulled her into his arm. "You remember my friend Alfred."

She nervously shook her head.

"No? How could you forget?"

"She was very young the last time I saw her," Alfred said. "You look well, Antigone."

Antigone turned to her father and held on to his sleeve. "Father, I need you to come with me. There's something I want to buy."

"In a moment, my dear, I'm busy now."

"But—"

"Don't worry, the businesses will remain open for a while, but I have something important to talk about with my friend first. Wait for me with your brother, okay? I'll be with you soon."

Once Antigone had left, Alfred wore a grim mask and asked, "What is your daughter doing here, Bertwin?"

"What she is meant to do," he said. "Fedor will need fresh alliances to strengthen his arm, and it's never too early to start."

"You can't be serious. You bring her with you at a time like this? Heading to what we are heading to?"

"Don't be so soft. You have a bad habit of always seeing the peril in things but not the opportunity. Now, try to see things from my eyes for a change: Many are gathering where we're going, and we're all aligned together for a change. *Aligned* underneath Valdes's banners, that is. There will be plenty of suitable candidates for me to choose her a companion from, and there will be plenty of talk. And when the right opportunity arises, I'll be able to seal the deal overnight. Don't misunderstand me, my friend, I'm not throwing my daughter to the wolves, and I will choose the best match I can for her."

"You mean for the future of your son."

"For her, for my son, and for all Ualky. Everybody wins. I need fresh alliances, and blood ties make the best bond… I told you already, Alfred, I've bet everything I have on this. If all goes well, then I will return home with renewed strength and enough spoils to keep my enemies at bay long enough to rebuild what's lost."

Having given his speech, Bertwin then relaxed back in his chair like a man in control.

"As for what we were talking about," Bertwin added, "perhaps I exhausted my breath for nothing. This wishful thinking of yours is but a flower planted in winter, and you know it. If you yourself had thought it stands a shred of a chance, then you would not have kept it a secret in the first place."

* * *

Volk was in a cheerful mood for a change.

He laughed and joked loudly as he led the way down a street with some urgency, his arm wrapped around a young woman.

When Agatha saw him, she changed direction and went after him. She came from behind him and laid her hand on his shoulder, stopping him.

"Volk."

His face darkened in an instant, and he attempted to shake Agatha off before she might ruin what he had worked so hard to achieve. "What? I'm busy, I'm busy, I can't talk right now."

She stopped him again. "Hold it right there. I need you back in your wagon, and I need you to stay there."

"What? Why?"

"We're to leave at dawn."

"What are you talking about, woman? We only just got here."

"These are your earl's orders."

The woman he had with him didn't need to hear a word more. She teared herself from his arms and hissed, "I thought you said you were the earl of the Toic."

With a sweaty face, Volk faked a laugh and attempted to salvage what he could from what Agatha had ruined. "What? No, no, no, I said the earl is my brother."

She raised an eyebrow. "Your brother?"

"Yes, he's like a brother to me. Wait, where are you going?"

She walked away, not looking back.

"Hold on, what about dinner?"

Agatha grabbed him by his shirt before he might go after the woman. "Did you not hear me?"

Volk shook her arm off and roared, "You see what you did?"

"Yes. Now, stop fooling around and get back to your wagon. Where are Teyrnon and Natir, weren't the three of you together?"

"How should I know! They took off somewhere as soon as we arrived and didn't tell me a thing."

She shoved him out of her way. "Fine, I'll look for them. You go back and tell the same thing to everyone you see on your way."

* * *

Natir was still shaken by what had happened when she came across a little girl.

She had beautiful and messy chestnut hair, and her face bore strong resemblance to Aina. Natir couldn't help but stare at her as she walked and thought to herself that this must be what Aina will look like when she's nine years old or so.

The little girl was crying loudly, and her little hand was holding on to the dress of a skinny woman with a face marred with tiredness and misery, repeatedly calling her, "Mommy."

But the one who was holding the little girl's arm was not the woman. Instead, it was the old and creepy-looking man standing before her.

Something felt odd about this scene.

Natir stopped and pretended to check the merchandise of a booth while she eavesdropped on the trio, and soon enough she felt a shock run through her so violently that a gasp caught in her throat when she realized what was happening:

The woman was all but negotiating the sale of her daughter to the old man.

Right before her eyes, she saw the woman accept the few coins the man gave her, and the deal was sealed.

Natir uttered in a small voice as the woman passed beside her, "Did you really sell your own daughter?"

The woman paid her words no mind and continued her way as if she had not heard her, while Natir kept turning her face between the woman's back and the little girl, who cried her eyes out as she was dragged away, apologizing for whatever childish misbehavior that came to her mind and begging her mother to come back.

The little girl's pleas ripped Natir's heart apart, and anger poisoned her breaths.

She ran after the mother as she decided in the heat of the moment to intervene and talk some sense into that heartless woman.

Chapter 7

CARNIVAL OF THE ROTTEN II

"Hey! Hey, you!"

Natir followed the woman but for a couple stores down the street before the woman rounded a corner and entered one of the businesses, Natir just a few steps behind.

The sudden change in scenery astounded her from her first step in there. Natir stopped near the entrance, taking in her surroundings.

It was a gambling-house.

The game tables were surrounded by players cheering and cursing aloud as they gambled away piles of coins. At every table, there was someone who wore a weird mask concealing part of their face, running the game.

A man enshrined with handsomeness sang from within a sizeable bird cage with an astounding voice.

Two women, perfect twins and perfect in looks, lay on bulky vinic cushions, making love to one willing patron after another.

Young waitresses strolled back and forth, serving the guests' every need and charming the men with their false smiles.

Great fireplaces made of clay in the shapes of women contorted in unabashed ecstasy had been strategically positioned throughout the place to keep every inch of the business summer-warm, and magnificent oil-lamps, just as salacious, illuminated the hall like daylight.

Natir's eyes returned to the woman she had followed, and she saw her take a seat at a table set for two players.

The woman's opponent was a sight to behold.

He sat like an unchallenged king behind a large, sheet-covered box at the center of the hall.

Bellied and shirtless, he boasted red hair primped like the wool of a sheep and a chest spangled with the same. His half-a-foot-long beard stood firm like a piece of wood glued to his chin, and his lips were full and painted like a woman's.

On the upper half of his face, he wore an engraved copper mask with an ugly, six-inch silver nose protruding from it, and in his arms he held a great lizard that he pet. Behind him stood a bodyguard wearing a similar mask but with a much smaller nose.

A hint of a familiar sweet scent aroused Natir's senses, causing her to frown.

She chose against talking with the woman just yet and decided instead to watch them. Natir zigzagged her way through the attendees as she slowly approached the game table and observed from a short distance.

The sight her new angle had revealed could only cause her stomach to churn.

The man's belt was burdened by pouches of money, and his throne was the bare back of a half-nude woman, a slave by the looks of her, one who neither her youth nor fair looks could save from him propping her down on all fours to suffer beneath his weight and who had been like that long enough for the skin of her knees to scrape and mark the floor with red stains…

It didn't take much for Natir to figure out the game: The players would place their wagers, throw three dice in a cup and flip it on the table, and the outcome decided the winner.

"What would your pleasure be?" a waitress stole her attention.

"What?"

Smiling, the waitress made an elegant motion to show Natir the cups she had on her tray. "Would you like something?"

Natir took her eyes off the waitress and back onto the game and said in a small voice, "Yes. Do you smell a candle?"

The waitress raised an eyebrow. "Yes?"

"Me too… Thank you."

The waitress looked baffled at first, but she went on with her work and didn't bother to throw a second thought at what every crazed person that walked into this place had to say.

Natir stole herself a few moments to slowly look from one side of the hall to the other, to reaffirm what she had suspected. The sweet scent was surely there, but not a single candle was in sight.

In a manner of only a few games, the woman had lost all her money and burst into tears, while the other player bobbed his head at her with disgust and ordered her to leave his table.

The woman was about to stand up when Natir appeared behind her, laid her hand on the woman's shoulder and pushed her back down on the seat.

Startled, the woman's face shot up at Natir.

"What's the game?" Natir asked with a grimace.

"What is this?" the man asked. "Are you a friend of hers? Or are you here to play?"

"What's the game?"

He eyed Natir up and down then held the dice in his palm and showed them to her.

"Three dices," he explained. "You roll them, and the result can be anywhere from three to eighteen. If you get a total of ten or more, you win. Anything less and the game keeper wins."

"So, all I need is to get the upper half of the possible results. Is that right?"

"*Well*, that's how the game is usually played. If you want to play it like that, then go to another table and any one of these losers will help you out. But not at my table," he said and made himself more comfortable. "With me, all you need to win is six."

"How generous of you. Why?"

He shrugged. "The goddess of luck favors me, and I almost never lose. That's why I'm the biggest nose in this place." He poked at the giant nose of his mask and laughed.

Natir said with disgust, "Yes, why shouldn't she? One look at you and I can tell she must be on her bed lusting for you right now."

He leaned forward and hissed, "Look, are you here to play or just waste my time? If you don't show me your money soon—"

Natir flashed her silver coin in front of him, causing him to go silent mid-sentence.

"Oh! Big gambler we've got here? I like that," he intoned and wagged his tongue back and forth, licking his upper lip.

"No," she said, "I do trust in luck…but I never gamble."

She placed her coin on the table before the stunned woman.

He gave Natir an odd look then turned to the bodyguard. Both men laughed.

"Women! They say one thing and do another."

"Are we going to play or tell jokes all night?" Natir said.

In response, he put his lizard on his shoulder, smacked his palm loudly onto the table, matching her bet, then toyed with the dice in the palm of his hand.

"You want to play with me? *Let's play*." He threw the dice in the cup.

They stared still at one another, neither of them blinking nor backing off, and the noise of the dice rolling inside the cup was all they could hear anymore.

"I'm going to melt your little coin and add it to my nose."

"Or I'm going to make your nose a whole lot smaller."

He flipped the cup on the table, and Natir swiftly set her hand atop of his so that he couldn't flip it.

He met her scowled gaze with a smirk, then he snickered. "What, you want to be the one to flip it?" he asked.

Slowly, he took his hand back then raised both his palms up and said with the confidence of a king, "All you needed to do was *ask*."

Natir offered him a sweet smile in return.

She took small, elegant steps to the side and stood between

him and the woman. Then, she played her drama.

With her eyes and smile set on him, she put her hand back on the cup, but then, instead of flipping it, she slowly shifted her hand to the edge of the table, feeling delighted by the way his gaze followed her hand and what changes her little motion brought to his face.

Suddenly, Natir groaned and flipped the table over with both hands.

Both players were shocked. The man jumped to his feet, but he stumbled on the slave he was sitting on and fell over while the female gambler leapt back, shirking; the commotion sent every face in the hall turned towards them to see what had happened.

Beneath the table, a little boy hid with a candle and a needle in his hands.

Natir quickly seized the boy by his shirt with her left, and with the other she grabbed his hand —the one that had the needle— and forced it upwards, showing it to all.

"It's a trick!" she shouted. "That white sheet concealed a hole in the table, and this little piece of shit hides underneath it and flips the dice from below with this."

The man's face was made of sweat. He stammered, "How did you know?"

Out of nowhere, a jug of wine broke against his face, shot at him by the woman whom Natir had followed.

"CHEATEERRR!" the woman screamed with all her voice, her face a mask of fury and her forefinger pointing him out like a murderer.

Chaos erupted in an instant as an enraged crowd ganged up on the gambler and his bodyguard, with the woman leading the charge and clawing at his face and his chest with her fingernails.

His lizard crawled in a hurry over the floor to escape, but it was trampled beneath the fighters' shoes and its belly exploded like a bag of water, splattering its guts all over the floor.

Natir remained where she was, smiling and watching the man get what he deserved, and she could not have followed all the hits that came at him even if she had a third eye to her face.

The boy crawled on the floor, aiming for the silver coin, but before he could snatch it, Natir placed her foot over it.

She crouched down, took the coin and wagged it meanly in his face. "That's mine, kid… Run. Run *now*."

The boy took off running. Natir straightened back up and kissed her coin before she put it back in her dress.

A man darted in front of her, causing Natir to stagger backwards to avoid him, but she stumbled on something under her heel and almost fell over.

She looked down and realized that she had stepped on one of the pouches the man had on his belt.

There was no time to think; the town guards were about to barge in, Natir could already hear their voices at the door. She had to make up her mind in the heat of the moment.

Her face darted face left and right, making sure no one was looking, and she swiftly snatched the pouch and hid it in her palms just as the guards swarmed into the place and ran past her.

The yells were deafening. The town guards broke up the fight and did not need to ask twice what had happened, not with all the accusations and unified finger-pointing.

They arrested the man and his bodyguard and dragged them out by their arms.

Natir followed the battered man with her eyes; he was gasping for air through his bloodied mouth, his legs kicking tiredly, and his face was marred by bruises and cuts.

Out of breath, he cursed Natir as he was dragged away, "I'll kill you for this, I'll kill you, I'll rape you in the street and kill you."

Natir responded by making a face and secretly dangling the pouch of money for him to see.

The man went berserk. He groaned and revolted in the guards' arms, prompting one of them to curse and hit him with a metallic bar that knocked him unconscious before they all disappeared behind the door.

The woman approached Natir and asked, mending her tawdry dress, "How did you know?"

"I thought I recognized the setting."

"What?"

She turned to the woman. "Men love to talk when they're happy. Suffer underneath their bodies long enough, and you will hear things you wouldn't believe." Natir then pulled the woman's hand and put the pouch of money in it. "Go buy back your daughter."

"What?" The woman was stunned. She opened the pouch and stared with awe at all the bronze coins in there. She asked cautiously, "Are you...giving this to me?"

"Go buy back your daughter," Natir repeated. "Never do something like that again."

She gave Natir an odd look at first, then her expression changed to that of a woman about to burst into tears of gratitude.

"Yes. Yes, I will. Thank you. Thank you. My lady, I don't even know your name, but with all my heart I pray, may the gods be with you every step of the way. Thank you."

She patted the woman's hands between hers and headed to the door, feeling a wave of relief and goodness sweeping through her. Then, just as she was a step away from walking out, she looked back and saw that the woman had taken a seat at another table to gamble.

Natir could not believe it. She charged over to the woman. "Hey?"

"Oh, yes?"

"Shouldn't you be going after your daughter?"

"Yes, I said I will."

"You should be doing it now!"

"I'll do it in a moment, what's the difference?"

A man said, "Woman, you are interrupting the game."

Another followed, "The wagers are set."

Natir glared at the woman with anger and disbelief burning in her eyes. She tried to snatch the pouch of money back from the table, but the woman was faster and had secured it in her lap before Natir can touch it.

"Hey! That's my money," the woman burst out with a face

maimed with anger. Her fist shot at Natir's hands as Natir tried to wrestle the pouch back.

"I only gave it to you so that you can—"

"You gave it to me, now it's mine. I'll do with it as I want!"

"Your daughter!"

"I told you, I'll get her in a moment!"

"Your daughter is in someone else's hands! Don't you care?"

"What does it got to do with you?"

"That's not what I gave you the money for—"

"So, you gave me a few coins, and now you think you can tell me what to do! What, you want me to worship you? What is wrong with you?"

"Me? I'm not the one who—"

"I did say thank you, didn't I? What more do you want? Now, leave me alone," she screamed as she slapped Natir's hand off and jumped away, holding the pouch tightly to her chest.

Natir charged after her, but the men interfered to the favor of the woman and got in between them.

"Woman, back off!" one man said as he gave Natir a push.

"She doesn't want to talk to you, you mind leaving her alone?"

"If you gave it to her, then it's her money."

"What do you want from her?"

Natir looked at them then back at the woman, staring daggers at her. She had never regretted helping someone as much as did then, nor could she comprehend how the woman could change into such an ugly person so quickly. It was like stepping on the tail of a dog.

Such was the woman's addiction, and underneath her skin there was a violence with a dagger in its hand.

A man came in front of Natir, much too close, and glared down at her.

He said, with his head tilting from side to side and a smutty twist on his lips like a hooligan looking for trouble, "Do we have a problem here, small tits? Hm? Because if we do…"

Her chest heaved as she glared back at him. "No. No problem at all," she said, breathing fire on her lips.

With the bitter taste of utter disgust tainting her mouth, Natir motioned at the woman with her head. "Have fun with your friends. *Have lots of fun.*"

Natir turned on her heel and headed out. Her hands shook violently as their foul jeers and mockery followed her out the door. Anger at herself had hardened into a stone in her chest, feeling that she had made a complete fool of herself.

Chapter 8

DIVA'S COMB

Every breath she took was fire.

Natir walked at a brisk pace. She felt horrible and wanted nothing more than to leave this place.

As if what had happened with her so far wasn't enough, the lewd looks and cat-calling she was getting from every man in her way had only made her feel worse. It made her feel like a piece of meat up for grabbing.

Just as Natir rounded another corner and the street where it all started was in sight, a short old man with a bent cane, who had been leaning his back against a wall before she passed by him, suddenly decided to try his luck with her.

He pushed off the wall and rushed after Natir. "Why, hello there."

Natir glowered at him with a momentous turn of her face, but she did not stop or respond.

"H...hold on for a moment... Don't you look lovely tonight... What's your name? Young...young woman, are you in a hurry?"

"Yes."

"Going somewhere?"

"Yes!"

"Where to?"

She lost her temper and burst out, "What do you want?"

The old man was a true manifest of the words 'a walking heap of shit' in her eyes.

He was at least sixty years old and so skinny and short that he barely measured up to her chest. His head was bald—in fact, it was flat-out hairless. His left eye was smaller than the right. Weird blisters plagued his abnormally large forehead.

His eyes roamed shamelessly over her body with the dirtiest looks anyone had ever given Natir, and the only thing filthier than his attitude were the cheap rags he wore under his old cloak that stunk of alcohol and urine.

"I just so happen to see a lovely young woman all dressed up and ripe for a good time," he said, "but somehow seems to have ended up all by herself on a lovely night like this. And I couldn't help but to think what a waste that would be."

If the muscles of her face weren't so taut by her frown already, Natir's eyes would have popped out. She couldn't believe that a creature so gross and old enough to be her grandfather had actually expressed his interest in her so bluntly.

"What, fucking, lovely night you're talking about?" she yelled out of her mind. "Can't you feel the cold? My hands are ice."

"Straight to the point, I love that in a woman. Tell you what, why don't you join me for a short walk, and I will definitely think of something nice to warm up that lovely butt of yours, *heeyyy*?"

She slapped his hand off her hips. "Don't touch me!"

"You like to get spanked?"

"What? Keep, keep your hands off...what is wrong with you?"

"No need to be shy, I got what you're looking for right here. Why, I may not look like it now, but back in my day, I was quite the man, I chopped wood with just one hand."

"I said don't touch me!" she yelled and slapped his hand away.

Natir leaned down to his level and hissed with rage, "You lay your filthy hand on me just one more time, and I swear on Perun's heart I'LL BREAK IT."

"Why the temper? I only—"

"Now, you listen to me, *old man*. I had just about enough of you, I had enough of these people, I had enough of this whole vile place already. So, why don't you go stick your head in that snowbank over there to cool it off, and if that doesn't work, GO SUCK IT YOURSELF! Now, leave me alone."

She turned on her heel and left, not willing to waste a word more on the creep.

"Fine, be like that," he shouted. "Cheap slut, who do you think you are? You don't know who you're turning your back on. You'll regret this. You'll regret this sooner than you think."

She only shook her head with disbelief.

Once she made it back to the street and the worst was behind her, she took a moment for herself to calm down her nerves.

Natir patted her dress, worried that the old man may have

dirtied it, when suddenly she froze and felt a wave of dread run through her.

She looked down at the ends of her belt with panic then quickly spun around herself, searching the ground with her eyes and her hands rummaging around her sides.

Her comb was gone! Stolen right from under her nose.

Natir gasped as she realized who the culprit might have been. She turned around quickly and saw the old man still weakly making his way towards the other end of the alley.

"Hey! Hey you!" She hurried out after him. "Stop. I said stop!"

He pretended not to hear her.

The moment she grabbed him from behind, the old man swiftly ducked down and took off running, leaving Natir with nothing but his cloak in her grasp.

"STOP! THIEF!" she screamed and immediately chased after him.

His creepy laughter only inflamed the rage already burning in her chest as she chased him from one alley to the next, not seeing a thing in her way, unstoppable by the slippery ice and all the pedestrians and obstacles showing in her path.

"STOP HIM! THIEF, SOMEBODY STOP HIM!"

It astonished her how fast he was for a man of his age. Natir was giving it all she had and yet she was barely able to keep closing the gap between them.

"THIEF!"

Just as he was almost within arm's reach, the old man made

a sudden turn before Natir could give it a final push and grab him. She rounded the corner, racing after him at full speed, only to see in a flash of white light his cane coming straight at her face.

Natir was struck down and rolled twenty feet through the street, screaming. She crashed against a wall so hard that globs of snow fell from the roof.

Her hand to her pained face, Natir wailed with pain and heard him laugh at her.

"That's what you deserve, you dumb tramp, that's what you deserve." He took off running again.

The strike had brought tears of pain to her eyes and her sight had blurred, but the rage in her chest was so great that she could no longer care; even if she had lost an eye, she would still have gone after him.

Natir hurried to her feet and raced with the wind, going after him even harder than before and yelling filths and threats.

After a short chase, she stopped at a fork in the road, turning her face left and right among three streets without a clue as to which way he had gone.

Natir bent down, holding her knees and panting like a bull.

She couldn't believe it. He was gone. Disappeared without a trace, and so was her comb.

All of a sudden, a frightening thought flashed through her mind, forcing Natir to tolerate the tiredness and straighten up again.

Gasping lungsful of air and spinning around herself, she mumbled, "Where am I?"

Chapter 9

ADVERSARY

As she wandered around aimlessly, hoping to grasp a clue of how to go back to where she's supposed to meet with Teyrnon, Natir ended up on top of a pedway without knowing how she got there.

It had never occurred to Natir that bridge-like roads could be constructed in the middle of a town like this, and for what purpose?

From on top of it, she could see that it wasn't the only one. Similar structures were scattered around town, great arches rising from one place only to fall to another like wooden rainbows. They ran above the houses and busy roads, and they even connected to some buildings at their top floors.

Although it wasn't of great length, the pedway still fascinated Natir. It was wide and made of tree trunks split in half with rails on either side decorated by wooden statues glazed with frost.

"Make way, woman, make way quick!"

A man grabbed Natir from behind and pushed her out of the way. Startled, she turned around to see what was happening.

Beneath a white banner with ten golden arrows embroidered on it, a column of riders had taken up much of the width of the pedway. Natir grew anxious when the horses passed within her arm's reach and turned to look between them and the drop at her back.

Screaming off in the air, a small flock of women-of-the-night called for the riders' attention with laughter and flirtatious display, hoping to seduce some of the men to join them, but to no avail.

The women and the man who had pushed Natir didn't seem even slightly concerned about getting accidentally pushed over. It eased Natir's worries as she came to realize that the riders were all master horsemen. They knew what they were doing, and the possibility of her getting knocked over was slim.

"They have a better chance of luring the lord to their beds than these people," the man said, motioning at the women.

His comment drew Natir's attention to the riders. They looked nothing like the men from her clan, or Alfred's, or any other village she'd been to.

They marched in an organized manner, and their clothes were replicas of each other: a unified armor made of layers of thick wool topped by a bronze chainmail. Their shields, strapped to their backs, were round and made entirely of shiny bronze.

Their swords, which they didn't turn in to the town garrison, were single-edge curved blades instead of the wide double-edge swords of the Boii. And they all wore bronze helmets, something not many would do in winter as to not risk their brains freezing.

But what stimulated Natir's curiosity the most was that they all shared strong resemblance to one another. They were all vigorous with serious expressions. All of them were blond and of similar age with turned-up noses and sharp jawlines. Their cheeks were perfectly shaved and their faces beautiful like women.

All two hundred of them could have easily been brothers.

"Who are they?" she asked.

The man gave her a look. "Terans," he said, "the backbone of Lord Valdes's army."

She intoned an "Oh!", although it explained so little. She asked again, "They're not Boii?"

"They are. But the idiots think they are better than the rest of us or something. I've heard that a Teran would never take a companion from outside their clan."

"Why not?"

He shrugged. "Ask them. I even heard they'd exile anyone who would. The arrogant bastards… This must be the rear column, catching up with their friends."

His last comment alerted Natir. She asked, "Catching up? What do you mean catching up?"

"What?"

"Valdes's army isn't here in this town?"

"Does it look like that loutish brute is still here? He already left days ago."

The news troubled Natir; it could easily ruin her plan to have alone time with Alfred. She had to let Teyrnon know about this.

Just then her eyes caught sight of something familiar. She recognized Irenka's store below.

Her face brightened. She grabbed the man's arm before he could leave and asked with haste, "Sir, wait. How do I get down there?"

* * *

After a dozen more encounters filled with harassment, Natir finally made it back to her starting point.

Irenka sat next to the entrance, watching the passersby with her head resting against her fist, and she had spotted Natir walking down the street from a good distance.

She raised an eyebrow and called out, "What are you doing back here?"

Natir froze like a child caught in a fib. Her hopes to sneak by unnoticed were shattered. "Oh, hi, I, um—"

"Did you see Teyrnon? What did he think of your new looks?"

"Actually, I was on my way now to see him."

"What?" Irenka frowned.

She got off her seat and approached Natir slowly and with such a glare in her eyes, it made Natir swallow against the knot in her throat.

"What does that mean?"

"Well, I kind of lost my way, and, um, I've found my way back here only just now."

"*Lost, your, way?*" she hissed, rage building in her chest. She grabbed Natir's arm and forced her to turn. "It's right there!" Irenka yelled. "How can you possibly lose your way?"

"Look, what happened was—"

"You can see it from over here. What, you can't follow your own eyes? What is wrong with you?"

"I know, I just, you see, there was this short old man and he—"

"You have any idea how long the man has been waiting for you? Hurry up and go already." She gave Natir a push. "Go. Move your legs!"

"Yes, I'm going, I'm going!"

"And keep your back straight. I said keep it straight. Walk like a woman, curse you!" Irenka yelled and buried her face in her palms.

*   *   *

The tavern, located at a thoroughfare, was a business with no windows and had a narrow entrance on either side veiled by beaded curtains.

Natir stole herself a moment to wipe her face and try not think of the terrible time she had on her way here. She sucked in a breath and was about to walk inside when Irenka's words ran through her head like an insult to her pride.

"*Walk like a woman, curse you.* Hah!" she mumbled like a child.

It was very irritating. Natir couldn't help but to prove a point, even if Irenka wasn't there and it was only to herself.

She mended her hair and dress with her hands, arched her back, then she strutted into the bustling tavern with one foot leading the other like she was walking on a narrow log.

Her hips rocked left and right, a fake smile adorned her lips, her left palm set on her side with feminine confidence while her right arm shot wildly into the air like she intended to snap her fingers.

Natir had finally gotten serious, and she was going to show Teyrnon that she could top Irenka at her own game. She was guaranteed to turn more than a few heads with every step she took…

* * *

Teyrnon was bored to tears by then, and it manifested on his body with fatigue.

He had his empty cup balanced on its edge between his finger and the table, trying to spin it around… It didn't work, the cup dropped onto the floor, and he didn't find it in himself to lean down and pick it up.

"Still waiting?"

Teyrnon raised his face to the servant who put his cup back on the table for him.

She was a young brunette with short hair and a slender build who had approached his table several times before.

She wore a lilac tunic and a leather necklace with an earthly sigil for protection and good luck engraved on the bone she had attached to it. Her lips were painted pink, and the opening of her light dress was a bit too wide, allowing Teyrnon to have a momentous glance onto the brilliance of her chest as she leaned forward.

Teyrnon couldn't help but to think she looked too good for a slave and dressed too well for her class, too. But then again so was every slave assigned to a business in Wenclas, who were hand-picked to outmatch the prettiest women one had back home.

"Two more drinks and I'll be the one you're waiting for," she said with a wink when she straightened back up and slightly swayed her body as her hand entrapped the empty tray flat against her side.

Teyrnon chuckled and nodded his head. "Yes. Yes, you probably will."

Unable to remember if he had paid for the last drink or not, he put a coin on the table and pushed it to her anyway, not regretting it for a moment if it turned out to be a tip too generous instead.

"No more drinks for me, I guess," he said.

She put her palm atop his hand before he could take it back and bent down to meet his eyes.

"My master will be disappointed by your words," she said, "selling more drinks is what he trusts me to do. What's more, *I* will be even more disappointed."

"Why would you?"

"Because…" She let out a beautiful breath on her lips as her little palm swept across her chest—pretending to fix her dress's shoulder while she secretly pulled on the opening to reveal her gorgeous cleavage to his eyes—as she murmured like a true siren, "I was *thinking*, I might just have one more drink I'd like to serve you."

Teyrnon stared, hypnotized by the alluring sight.

She set her elbow on the table and rested her cheek on her

palm, prompting him to turn his gaze to her eyes again. "And you don't need to worry about paying for the *wine* I intend to serve…" she said with an inviting smile, then signaled him with her eyes and whispered, "There's a room in the back, behind the wide table."

Teyrnon needed a moment to claim himself from the depths of the magic in her eyes. He reached for his pouch and pushed another coin to her. "I appreciate the offer, but—"

With a lean motion, she masterfully snatched the coin into her palm before anyone might see it and straightened up.

"What offer?" she teased. "I was just saying *I'm going that way.*" She bit on her lower lip in an unmistakable hint before she left.

Teyrnon turned around in his seat, following her with his eyes, and saw her look back at him and narrow her gaze just before she disappeared behind a door.

He wiped his face with his palm and turned his face between the business's entrance and the door of his mystical enchanter. The drinks he had had weakened him to temptation, and waiting for Natir had taken much, much longer than he had anticipated.

Teyrnon shook his head. His patience had finally run out, and he decided to go look for Natir.

His timing couldn't have possibly been worse; Teyrnon left through one door just as Natir entered from another.

Natir's enthusiasm faded as she walked slowly between the tables, searching for Teyrnon with her eyes. When she couldn't find him, Natir decided it was best to grab a seat and wait as he surely wasn't going to leave her alone in this place and would return soon.

She sat at a corner to minimize the unwelcomed interest and tapped her fingers to the table, hoping to see Teyrnon walk in.

Natir huffed with impatience. She leaned her elbow against the table and traced the line of her eyebrow with her finger while keeping an eye on the entrance when suddenly she caught a glimpse of something that shocked her.

She was on full alert as she gave her whole attention to the loud and cheerful group of four men who entered the tavern, trying to ascertain what she thought she had seen until Natir was absolutely sure that her eyes hadn't tricked her.

In the hands of one of them was her stolen comb!

Natir didn't waste a moment. She approached their table. "Excuse me, sir."

The man who had the comb was so indulged in the conversation with his friends, it seemed he failed to hear her over the bursting laughter.

She raised her voice, "Excuse me!"

He threw Natir a glance from over his shoulder and waved his hand, dismissing her. "No need to apologize," he said and resumed talking to his friends.

Insulted, Natir tapped his shoulder. "Sir? Sir, I'm talking to you."

"What?" he barked at her.

"That's—"

"Woman, you can see that I'm talking to someone, can't you?"

"I only—"

"Look, I saw what you're selling, and I'm not interested, all right?" he interrupted with disgust. "Now, stop being a bitch about it and go rub your skinny hips on someone else."

Her jaw hung open whilst the man shook his head with disbelief and continued his conversation, totally ignoring her.

Flushed with fury and impatience, Natir quickly laid her hand on top of his drink and pushed it out of his reach when he attempted to grab it.

She then leaned down to his level and hissed, barely able to contain the anger rising in her chest, "I'm trying to tell you, *sir*, that's my comb you've got in your hand."

"What?"

"I said, that's my stolen comb in your hand."

Enraged by her words, he immediately got up, knocking the wooden stool back in the process, and glared down at Natir.

"Woman, did I hear you right? Did you just accuse me of stealing?"

"I didn't say it was you who stole—"

"Then what was it that you said? Do you even think before you talk, bitch, or does shit ooze out of that anus in your face on its own?"

A man of the wild. There was little room to reason with him.

He towered a head taller than most men, and his build was easily on par with Gull's. He seemed to be in his thirties. His clothes were rugged and topped by a gray cloak. His face was scarred and had a naturally vicious expression, and his black beard was braided on either side.

"Listen, I'm only here to ask you, very respectfully, to please return my comb," said Natir.

"*Your* comb?"

"Yes, my comb. Look, I don't know how it ended up in your hands, and I'm not saying that you stole it, but that is still my comb and I want it back."

"And what makes you think it's yours?"

"Because I'm telling you, it's mine. It's a gift that I hold very dear to me and I would never—"

"Oh, so it's a gift now?"

"You're not listening."

"No, it's you who's not listening." He leaned his face down at her. "The comb is mine. Or did you really think you can just walk here, shake your cheap butt and babble a few lies, and I will...what? Give it to you, just like that?"

She hissed back, "That's my comb. It wasn't even an hour ago that it was stolen from me, and one way or another, I will get it back. How did you even get your hands on it?"

"That's none of your business."

"It is my business."

"Your business is in your rear, bitch. Now, fuck off."

"I'm not moving a step from here until I get my comb back."

"My patience with you is running thin. Fuck off, mouth of filth, before I drag you naked out of here and smack your butt in the street."

"Look, I'm not here to fight with you, I just want—"

"Fight me?" A laugh escaped him. "Why, by all means, please do! Show me how a woman fights. Come on, show me. What are you going to do, splash my face with your tit-milk? You're going to squeeze my cock dry between your legs?"

Natir raged, "Do you even know how to talk like a normal person? Give me back my comb!"

"For free! Just like that?"

"All right then...all right." Her hands shook as she hysterically searched her dress for the coin and slapped it onto the table. "There! I'll buy it back from you."

He slapped the coin back at her. "Does it look like I want your dirty money, you whore?"

She yelled, "Then what is it that you want?"

The man took a step in and, smirking, waved the comb in front of Natir. "You want this comb?" He quickly raised it out of her reach when Natir tried to snatch it. "Hm? Do you really want it?"

"Yes! Give it back."

"All right then, if you want it so badly, then I expect nothing less than to hear an immediate *yes* on your cute little whore-lips when I tell you to pay for it."

"I've already offered you all the money I have! What more do you want?" she screamed.

"*Oh*, what's up with the temper? That's not a way to ask for a favor, now is it?"

She hissed, "Just tell me what you want."

He leaned his face closer at hers and demanded, "What I want is to see you write the word *woman* on your forehead then get down on all fours and lick the balls of every man in this place like the bitch you were born to be. Then, you will get up on this table and dance naked for me until I'm satisfied. Do it. And I'll give it to you."

Natir glared back at him as her cheeks reddened with anger.

Forget how little the world thought of women, this man was on a whole different level. *This* was the enemy of all women.

Natir was sure by now that he wasn't going to give her her comb back, not even if she turned her skin to gold.

He was glaring back at her with lidless eyes and a dirty smirk on his mouth when he suddenly applied more pressure to his thumb and the comb snapped in half, causing Natir to gasp.

Like in slow motion, she watched with eyes filled with dismay as her comb dropped at her feet in two pieces, and it hurt her worse than if a knife had cut through her flesh.

"Too late," he said amidst the laughter of his friends. "You should've taken the deal, bitch."

Her chest heaved out of control.

Anger consumed Natir so swiftly that she could no longer breathe, instead choking on her own emotions as she raised her head and landed her smoldering eyes on his smug face like a woman ready to commit murder.

"What's up with that look on your face? You're going to cry on me now, is that it? You're going to cry, little girl?"

His friends laughed. "Boohoo, he broke my toy."

"Come here, shake your hips on my lap. I'll buy you a comb."

"She's going to cry!"

Not saying a word, Natir turned on her heel and rushed out of the tavern with the four men's wild laughter and insults ringing in her ears.

On her way out, Natir snatched a cup from one of the tables, spilled its contents onto the floor and mumbled quietly to herself. "You want me to fight like a woman? All right, I'll show you, I'll show you exactly how a woman fights, no need to beg me for it, you pig."

She went outside for but a short time before returning to the tavern again, holding a filled cup in her hand. She inspected the servants with her eyes as they walked around, looking for a proper candidate.

Natir waited patiently by the entrance until the servant she had chosen came close enough to notice her and crocked her finger at the woman, signaling her to come closer. "You."

The servant, the brunette with a lilac dress, approached Natir with a cup of beer balanced on the wooden tray she had in her hands.

"Yes?"

Natir put her cup on the woman's tray.

"Take this to the man at that table, the one with a gray cloak, and tell him it's a gift *frommm*…" Natir played her forefinger in the air, taking her pick. She pointed out the biggest man in the room. "That man."

The servant raised an eyebrow. She was overtaken by awkwardness at first, but when she realized that the cup Natir had given her was full of piss, she grimaced.

"You want me to get whipped? What are you trying to do?"

Before the words were fully out of her mouth, Natir had already unhooked the hair extension braid Irenka had dressed her with and pushed it into the servant's hand.

"For your trouble."

The woman turned her face between Natir and the braid with shock. She then flashed Natir with the smile of a thousand roses and offered her the other cup. "Would my lady care to enjoy a drink while she waits?"

"Why, thank you."

Natir accepted the beer. She then leaned her back against the wall, crossed her ankles and wrapped one arm over her chest as she watched and waited.

She saw the servant take the cup of piss to the man who broke her comb and deliver him the message. The man wore a suspicious look and kept turning his face between the servant and the big man Natir had pointed out as the sender.

When the servant left and he brought the cup close to his nose, the scent alerted him to what was in it, and he instantly flew into a rage. He slammed the cup to the table, headed towards the big man without delay, and punched him in the face.

A vicious brawl erupted and swiftly spread throughout the

place as the friends of either side jumped into the fight, all while Natir remained standing by the entrance, relaxing and enjoying her drink and occasionally making funny faces or looking away every time someone received a vicious blow.

The hero whom she put her faith in to extract revenge for her in a mere blow or two wasn't doing all that great. In fact, the two men were equally matched despite the difference in size. But when the man who broke her comb was knocked face-down on the floor, Natir immediately seized her chance.

She ran to where he lay, snatched a chair on her way and smashed it onto the back of his head when no one was looking.

Natir then took a wide step, walking over him, retrieved the cup and poured her piss all over his head.

"That was my comb," she said hatefully, dropped the empty cup on him and walked away.

All of a sudden, she gasped. His hand had shot out, taking Natir by complete surprise as he grabbed her ankle.

"I should've known," he groaned.

He then quickly pulled her in, causing Natir to fall on her hips screaming.

Natir panicked and tried to free her ankle, but he had quickly drawn her in and, roaring like a mad man, got up and swung her around over the floor and into the air by her ankle before throwing her away.

Natir screamed as she crashed against a wall and onto a table.

She got up in a hurry and jumped back at him when, out of nowhere, the town's guards swarmed into the tavern and ganged up on the fighters.

It took six men to keep Natir and her foe apart as the two of them pelted their fists into the air and shouted filths, trying to get a hold of one another.

Chapter 10

AGNARR

Irenka face-palmed herself. "You have got to be kidding me."

"What?" Teyrnon asked.

He was back at Irenka's place, talking to her in front of the store to inquire about Natir.

"You didn't see her on your way here?" Irenka asked.

"Well, no. Why? Did she just leave?"

"Of course not. I sent her on her way a *long* time ago, then she came back and said that she lost her way and that she was going to see you then."

"When was that?"

"Not too long ago."

"Irenka?"

"What, does it really look like I'm playing a game with you?" She lost her patience. "I'm serious. Look, I did what you asked me for and more. I cleaned her up, I dressed her, I fixed her looks like you wouldn't believe, and I even taught her a trick or two, then I sent her on her way to see you and perfectly described the place for her. It's just down the road, for Veles's sake. What more do you want me to do, hold her hand?"

He backed off. "I understand, I understand, please calm down, I was just asking."

"Are you sure you two didn't cross ways? She has an ivory dress now and a hair braid, too. You should have still recognized her."

Teyrnon turned his face between Irenka and the other end of the street, unsure what to do.

"So, you think she's there now?" he asked.

"Unless she lost her way again, then yes, she should be, and if she has a brain between her ears, then she will stay there and wait."

"Well, I guess I should go back and look for her then."

"Yes, I imagine that you should."

He turned to leave but hesitated and asked Irenka again, "Irenka, do me a favor, if by any chance you see her come back this way—"

"Seriously?" She raised an eyebrow.

"I'm just saying, you know. Just in case."

"Teyrnon, love, I've got just one question for you: With Morana's name on your tongue, where do you find these women?"

* * *

"You are one disgusting load your mother should have swallowed," he whispered.

"That's so funny coming from a face that can scare the *shit* out of a chamber pot," Natir whispered back.

He turned to her. "You better watch your back, bitch,

because once this is over, I'm going to look for you, and I'm going to batter your head onto the ground until your eyes pop out of your stupid face, and then I'm going to stick hooks through those limbs of fat at your chest and drag you down the streets by your tits."

She hissed back, "You just wait until I tell them how you stole from me—"

"Oh, I stole from you?"

"I'm going to piss myself laughing when I see you hung from a bridge by your balls before dawn, pig-face."

"BE QUIET, BOTH OF YOU," a guard yelled. "This is the last time I warn you."

"Yes, yes, whatever, big man," he mumbled.

After Natir and her opponent were identified as the ones who started the fight, they were put in chains and taken away by the town's guards, where the two of them soon found themselves standing in a grand hall before an empty, magnificent seat fit for a king.

Natir could not get over how opulent the hall was.

She easily killed time admiring her surroundings with her eyes, shifting her gaze from the expensive velvet fabric of the embroidered curtains, to the rustic candleholders made of bronze in the shape of tree branches, to the stone statues of wild beasts with sinister expressions and others of overly muscular nude men in poses just as violent, wielding their weapons as if they were charging at invisible foes.

The main seat and surrounding furniture were made of a

single piece of wood, each, and were engraved with such amazingly fine details depicting half-nude maidens encompassed by fascinating nature, even the curved benches—set five steps behind Natir and arranged around the main seat in half a circle—had figures of women holding musical instruments and swirls carved into their bases.

Natir's opponent, however, had far less patience. "Hey, how long am I supposed to keep waiting like this?"

The guard snapped, "Didn't I tell you to keep your mouth shut? Don't make me gag you."

"Why don't you come closer and talk like that to my face, you chicken."

Just then, the guards' leader returned to the hall and raised his voice, "All the accused, bow your heads."

Natir and her opponent stared blankly back at him.

He grimaced. "I said: *bow your heads*. And neither of you speaks unless you're spoken to."

Her opponent looked away and scoffed while Natir dropped her face and took the chance to mend her dress, hoping to charm her way out of this mess.

She heard the unsteady footsteps of someone heading towards the hall in a hurry. Once the newcomer entered, Natir caught a glimpse of his robes out of the corner of her eye as he aimed straight for the seat to assume his place, shouting on his way.

"What? What is it this time? This is the eighth time today."

"You may raise your heads."

When Natir looked up again, she was astonished to see the seat filled beyond its capacity by a man who was mostly made of belly.

The man had not suffered hunger a day in his life. He was so overfed that his belly dangled between his enormous thighs. Not a trace of his neck could be seen from behind his double-chin, and his breasts could put any woman to shame.

He smelled finer than a damsel appareled with roses and was overdressed with strikingly colorful garments of purple embroidered with shades of gold. His eyebrows were trimmed thin, his cheeks powdered, his thick fingers surrounded by at least twenty gold rings, and on his chest he wore a chain made of bricks of gold, each the size of an egg.

"Well?" the fat man demanded again. "Are you going to tell me what am I looking at or not?"

"Sire, it's a small matter of a fight in a tavern."

"That's it? That's what's so urgent that it can't wait until morning?"

The guards' leader leaned toward him and said under his breath, "Sire, the thing is, they are both outsiders and—"

The fat man scornfully waved his hand. "Yes, yes, yes. The new instructions and all of that." He then turned to Natir and her opponent. "All right, you two, will someone tell me what happened?"

Natir had no doubt in her mind who the fat man was. She quickly seized the initiative. "My lord, allow me to explain. This man—"

"Lord?" He raised an eyebrow, causing Natir to hesitate.

Her opponent mocked, "You idiot, that's not the lord of Wenclas. The lord is the skinny fellow with golden nipples."

"BE SILENT," the fat man roared. "I will not have the good name of our lord ridiculed by common filth under the very roof of my hall."

"Well, he is skinny, isn't he?"

"Well, uh—"

"And he got gold on his nipples, does he not?"

"QUIET." He hammered the seat's arm with his palm and leaned forward. "Look here, you, depending on how you behave yourself from here on, I may or may not let these rotten comments of yours slip unpunished, but be warned that this type of wordplay has no place in my hall. Dare to test my warning and you will know nothing but regret." He then turned to Natir. "As for you, woman."

"Yes?"

"I have little patience to educate those who don't bother to educate themselves, but out of the kindness of my heart, I will spare a moment to explain this real quick: I am not the lord. My name is Wilhelm the Kovaryk. I am the judge of Wenclas, and you will address me as *Sire* from now onward."

"Judge? But…" She hesitated.

"What? What is it? Don't just mumble with half-sentences! Finish what you've got to say properly."

Natir turned her face left and right then took a small step forward and asked, "Sire, forgive me, but you've just said that you're not the lord. How then can you judge us?"

"Ignorant!" Wilhelm said aloud. "This isn't the puny villages that the...the...well, the likes of you come from. You think that our lord has got time to look into every little conflict that happens by the dozens every hour of the day? Of course not. He's got more important things to do. That is why the task of resolving everyday conflicts was entrusted to my illustrious judgment, and I rule in the name of the lord. Is it clear to you now?"

Natir nodded.

"Respond!" Wilhelm said. "You don't just nod your head at me. Make your voice be heard."

"Yes, Sire."

"Good. Now, very briefly, I want you to tell me what happened."

Natir pointed at her opponent and burst out, "He stole my comb."

"Lying filth—" her opponent countered, both of them speaking at the same time.

"He had it in his hands, he stole it, and then he broke it—"

"No, no, no, don't listen to any of that, the cheap slut tried to scam me—"

"He did it on purpose, did...did you hear what he called me? His tongue is rot and smut—"

"The comb was rightfully mine—"

"If only you'd heard half the things he said to me, it would've made you want to spit in his face—"

"I was minding my own business when *she* intruded on my table and tried to trick me—"

"Lies, the comb was mine, I swear. But his accomplice, a short old man, he stole it—"

"First, she tried to seduce me, then—"

"They're in this together—"

Wilhelm buried his face in his palm while the guards' leader repeatedly shouted at them to be quiet and finally roared, "SHUT UP, BOTH OF YOU."

"…She pees in cups."

"I SAID SHUT UP!"

"A comb?" Wilhelm said after a pause. "You tell me that I had to leave my most foremost guests without their host and come all the way down here again, in the cold, and listen to this mess of a story, all because of a stupid *comb*?"

"He stole it from me!"

"She's lying!"

"ENOUGH! What is this? It's like I'm dealing with children! Enough about the stupid comb." He turned to the guards' leader. "And you, I thought you said this was about a fight in a tavern."

"It is, Sire. Apparently the two of them had an argument, then he started the fight."

"Oh, I started the fight? The fight which she caused?"

"I did not," Natir countered.

"You threw the first punch," the guards' leader affirmed. "We've got a witness who saw you."

"Is that so? And where is this witness of yours?"

"He's standing right there!" He pointed at a man who had been waiting quietly in a corner of the room.

Wilhelm called, "You there, the witness, step forward... Did you see who started it?"

"Yes, Sire."

"Good. Now, listen to my questions carefully and answer me: Did you actually see him throw the first punch? Did you see his face clearly, and was he the very same man standing before us?"

"Yes Sire, I'm absolutely certain, I got a good look at his face."

Natir's opponent headed towards the witness. "Is that right?"

The guards' leader shouted, "You there, stop!"

Two guards quickly drew out their weapons and intercepted him. "Hold still."

"Relax, you cunts," he said in between their swords, "I'm just going to ask the man a question." He then faced the witness. "You, did you just say that you are *absolutely certain* you saw my face?"

"I—"

"If you had had such a good look at my face, then I must have seen yours, too. Doesn't that sound right? But you know what's funny...?"

Overtaken by shock, Wilhelm stuttered, "Hey! HEY! What do you think you're doing? Stop him. That's...that's solid bronze, you fool."

Natir had gone speechless as she witnessed with eyes flung wide open how her opponent, like in a fairytale, groaned aloud and put on a spine-chilling show of strength as he pulled on the chain in his hands until it gave way and broke.

"I AM AGNARR THE ABARATHY."

He declared like a beast, unshaken by the guards who ganged up on him nor the swords pointed to his chest.

"I am the fang of my clan. The one who slay the earls of the Tsui, that was ME! The one who defeated the champion of the Grath and burned their homes to rubble, that was ME! ME!"

Natir had the 'oh shit' look on her face.

This wasn't just any man. This was 'somebody'. A hero from the realm of fame… And his hair was yet dripping with her piss!

"And I don't recall ever seeing you before," Agnarr said as he returned to the witness, "but if you say you remember seeing my face *for certain*, then it would only be proper *that I remember yours, too.*"

The witness was so afraid suddenly, he looked like he was about to faint.

"So, take a good look at my face, you skinny wimp, because I'm going to ask you one last time: Have you seen my face before?"

Chapter 11

A WOMAN WITHOUT A MARK

Teyrnon returned to find the tavern in havoc.

Few men were inside; they had taken over what tables and chairs they could find still in one piece and sat in separate groups drinking and murmuring among themselves while the business's few slaves went through the rubble to salvage what they could.

Teyrnon walked in, turning his head about looking for Natir, when he spotted the servant with the lilac tunic trying to pull a chair from under the broken wood.

"You need help with that?" Teyrnon offered.

When she spun around, her face was coated with a glistening sheen of sweat, but it only made her look more attractive.

"Oh, you came back," she said, wiping her forehead with the back of her hand.

"Let me get that for you."

She stopped him. "No, it's fine. I might get in trouble if you do… So," she waved her arm sarcastically, "help yourself to a seat, if you can find one."

"What happened?"

"The usual, only a little more intense tonight. It's nothing you don't get used to." She resumed her work. "You learn to hide in a corner and keep your head down until it passes."

"I see… Say—"

"The backroom is out of the question now." She looked up at him from where she had bent and added, "But it doesn't mean I can't sneak out later, if you don't mind the wait."

Her wink caused Teyrnon to chuckle with nervousness, and he couldn't come about a different approach to turn the woman down for the second time in one night.

"Actually, I'm looking for someone."

She resumed what she was doing and said with little interest, "You mean the woman you've been waiting for?"

"How did you know?"

"Why else would you wait so long? Certainly not for a good old friend. Well, as you can see, me and my friends are the only women around, but tell me what she looks like, maybe I've seen her."

"Well, um, let's see. She's about your age and height, and she's wearing a white, I mean, ivory dress—"

She froze with a stunned look on her face.

"Brown hair—"

The servant couldn't help but to crack a laugh.

She straightened up and turned to him. "Hazel eyes? Short hair, like mine? Has a wound to her waist and she covers it with Breuci art?"

"That's the one…" he said, but she just kept staring back at him with a devious smile. "So, you did see her?"

She crossed her arms over her chest and made a little motion with her head. "That's a very nice pin you've got there."

"Uh, thanks." It dawned on him a moment too late what she had meant. Teyrnon looked, stunned, from her to the pin at his chest. "Really?"

She shrugged. "I'm just saying that's a very, *very* nice pin. I can't help but to wish I had one just like it."

With a lot of hesitation, he took off the pin and offered it to her. "You can have it."

"Why, thank you. Aren't you both sweet and generous?" she said with a girlish sing-song tone as she admired her new pin, then a laugh escaped through her nose when she saw the look on his face. "What?"

"I just can't decide what you're really interested in, me or what I have?"

She snickered. "Why can't it be both? One more than the other, perhaps."

"Which one?"

With her hands joined behind her back, she lightly rocked her body and teased, "Care to find out?"

Teyrnon shook his head, smiling. "If the circumstances were different, I imagine that I would have." He asked again, "So, did you see her? You know where she went?"

"Did I see her?" She shrugged and waved her arm. "Who do you think caused all of this?"

His face went pale in an instant, and it took him a moment to find his voice again. "What...?"

* * *

Having learned what had happened to Natir, Teyrnon was so overwhelmed with worry that he couldn't think straight anymore.

He stepped out of the tavern and turned his head from one end of the street to the other, unsure what to do and where to look for her.

"Teyrnon!"

His tongue went numb. Agatha had spotted him, and she came towards him with a burst of urgency in her legs.

"Where have you been?" Agatha asked.

"I, um—"

"Where is Natir? Wasn't she with you?"

Teyrnon decided in the heat of the moment to keep what happened to Natir a secret and hopefully resolve the situation himself before things got worse.

"Uh, yes. Yes, she was."

"Good. I need her back at the convoy with everybody else, and make sure to tell her to stay there."

"What? Why?" he asked. "What happened?"

"Alfred's orders. Valdes and his men have already left, and we must leave after them first thing in the morning. We will not wait until the last moment and end up wasting time looking for everyone gone missing somewhere."

Teyrnon yelped, "Are you serious?" His mind raced. This could only add to the bad news he harbored.

"We've informed most of the men," she said, "but there are

a few still scattered around. Help me find them and then meet me back at the convoy in an hour."

"Agatha, wait!" He stopped her by her arm before she could leave. There was no hiding what had happened anymore; Teyrnon needed all the help he can get.

"About Natir. There's something you must know."

*   *   *

The witness stammered, "N...n...n...no."

Agnarr turned his ear to him. "What? I can't hear you."

"No." The witness turned to the judge and raised his voice with fear. "It's not him."

Wilhelm was enraged. "What do you mean it's not him? What then did we bring you here for?"

"It's not him. Not him. I've never seen this man before in my life."

"Well, if it wasn't him, then who was it?"

"It was...IT WAS HER."

"WHAT?" Natir yelped.

He pointed at her. "It was her. I saw it. She started the whole thing. It was all her."

The shock stole the words from Natir's mouth.

Agnarr patted the witness' cheek. "Vigilant man."

"Y...yes, sir. Thank you, sir."

Natir could not believe what had happened nor how quickly

the tables had turned on her. Meanwhile, Wilhelm nodded his head and muttered, "I see."

With all the ruckus Agnarr's revolt had caused, hardly anyone noticed the old guard who entered the hall amidst the broil and approached Wilhelm in a hurry.

The old guard had taken himself a place behind Wilhelm and whispered at the first chance he got, "Sire."

Wilhelm looked over his shoulder, surprised to see the old guard there. "Uh, yes, what is it?"

"A word, please."

"Oh, hold off for a moment, I'm just about done here." Wilhelm then turned his attention back to Natir and Agnarr. "Sooo, you are Agnarr the Abarathy? You look exactly as I thought you would." He cracked a laugh and resumed, "Well then, now that we've got to the bottom of this at last—"

Natir shouted, "Wait, what? You can't just let him get away with that."

"Get away with what?"

"He intimidated the witness, he forced him to spout lies."

"Nonsense!" Wilhelm brushed it off. "How can a witness be intimidated in my hall, and under my personal protection? It's utter ridiculousness."

"YOU'VE JUST SEEN HIM DO IT."

"All that I've seen and heard was a man asking a witness the very same question I asked, and the witness answered."

A small gasp escaped her. Natir realized a little bit too late that the scale of judgment had entirely tilted to her opponent's side before she could do anything about it.

Wilhelm said, "Now then, to wrap this matter up: You, the aggressor."

"Me?" Natir gasped.

"No, the guard behind you. Yes, of course I'm talking to you, your guilt has been proven, hasn't it—?"

"What guilt?" she retorted.

"Tell us your name and where you're from. Come on, come on, I don't have all night."

Natir looked about, so anxious that she had trouble keeping her chest from heaving in and out.

"My name is Natir," she answered. "I'm an Attee."

"Attee? Who are the Attee? Oh, an Alauni! Well, you've certainly traveled far from home, haven't you?" He cracked another laugh. "Well, Natir the Attee, you are a very lucky woman. Wenclas has decided to warm up to its guests in these cold winter days, so you don't have to worry about getting whipped or anything of the sort. Just tell us who your master is and we'll have him pay for the damages you caused and put this little mess behind us."

"I have no master, and I'm no slave."

"You got short hair."

"I was set free days ago," she said with a grimace. "I am not a slave anymore, and I will not be judged as one."

"Oh, I see, I see, that certainly explains the attitude."

The old guard interrupted Wilhelm again, "Sire, please, I must have a word with you."

"Hold off for a moment, I said." He turned back to Natir. "Very well, Natir. I will rephrase my question to your ego's delight: Tell us who *your man* is."

She hesitated. "I...don't have a man either."

Agnarr snorted, "Go figure."

"Shut your mouth!" she barked.

"Perhaps I jumped to conclusion," said Wilhelm. "Didn't your master set you free in order to take you as a companion? Did I presume wrong?"

"No, he didn't. I was only set free."

"You mean you managed to buy yourself? Or, how?"

"No, I...I was set free and that was it. What does it matter how?"

"Natir, slow down, I'm getting a little confused here. Are you trying to tell me that you're here all by yourself? Just what exactly are you doing in Wenclas anyway?"

Agnarr said, "Can't you tell just by looking at her?"

Her face darted towards him.

"Yes, well, this is still a hall of justice, Agnarr, and even slaves and sex entertainers are allowed to have their say, so let her speak for herself."

Provoked, Natir raised her voice, "I said I'm not a slave and I'm certainly not a sex entertainer. I am here with the Toic and we are just passing through."

"The Toic?" Wilhelm raised an eyebrow. "The Toic are heading to war. What do you have to do with them?"

"I'm one of them."

"I don't understand, didn't you say you're an Attee?"

"Well, I...I was born an Attee, but I'm about to become a Toic."

"About to? So, you're not a Toic as of yet?"

"Well, no, but—"

"Are you a Toic or an Attee? Make up your mind."

Some of the guards voiced into the conversation, "It's a simple question, woman."

"Who's the head of you?" another guard asked.

"Stop stalling. Show us your mark, stupid."

Natir was cornered. "I don't have one."

Wilhelm leaned forward, clearly his patience was being tested. "You have no tribal mark?"

"No, Sire, look, let me explain, the thing is I was too young to be celebrated before I became a slave—"

"You mean by the Attee?" Wilhelm interrupted.

"Yes."

"All right, I hear you. So, you're not an Attee either."

"Well, no, but by birth—"

"I understand, I understand." Wilhelm said, waving his hand, "All right then, show me your ex-master's seal and tell me where he is from."

She stammered, "I...don't—"

Before she finished answering, Wilhelm lost his patience and raised his voice. "First, you told me you're an Attee, then you told me you're a Toic, and now you say you don't have the mark of either of them. Not only that, but you don't even have the mark of your *own master* who you said freed you just *days ago*! What nonsense is this? Woman, who are you? Show me a tribal mark, a seal, a token, show me something, anything!"

"But I don't have anything."

He threw his arms in the air. "Who in the world doesn't have their mark? Who doesn't have people to vouch for their claim? How else can you prove that you are who you say you are?"

"I'll tell you who," Agnarr said. He approached Natir and jeered in her face, "A *tribeless whore*. A lower-than-filth, disowned, walking piece of fuck-meat who no one will put their mark on the likes of and has only come to this wealthy place and frilled herself like this in the hopes of finding herself buyer after buyer until her hands are loaded with so much bronze she cannot close her fingers and her rear with so much spurt it will run down her legs."

She hissed, "You are pure filth."

"What's your price, whore, a month of you for a copper?" he mocked.

"Tell them the truth, curse you."

Agnarr leaned at her shoulder to whisper, "The truth is whatever gets me out of this mess and flushes you down the drainage, stupid."

She revolted, "You son of a—"

"That's enough!" The guard behind Natir quickly intervened. He held her still by her upper arm before she could lay a hand on her foe.

"Pray that I never see you again," she said, glaring at Agnarr, "because with Morana's name on my tongue, I swear, I will make you pay for every word you've said."

Agnarr smirked and turned to Wilhelm. "It's just as I said, and we all know it," he called aloud. "You really think she's free? An Attee? A Toic? You're going to take her word on it? The word of a *woman*."

"Agnarr—" Wilhelm tried to interrupt.

"How else do you think they can wag their tongues around a man's piece the way they do if it wasn't for the lies they tell all day long?"

She breathed fire into her chest as the hall erupted with laughter.

"Nevertheless…" Wilhelm spoke aloud and waited for the laughter to tone down. "Nevertheless, none of that is a concern of mine. In fact, I just realized that at this particular time I should not care if she's free or slave or to which clan she specifically belongs to. All that matters is that she's clearly an outsider, and that by itself overshadows everything else for that the lord has ordered us with leniency to our guests."

Wilhelm then looked at Natir. "That was an unnecessary waste of time. Be thankful, Natir, for that if this had happened on any other day, the consequences for you would have been *very severe*. But by the grace of our lord, I will overlook your lies."

"I didn't lie!" she shouted.

"I will not entertain an argument that doesn't matter." He declared aloud, "As I just said, I care not who you are or to where you belong, except for that now I have no choice but to take you on your word and order you to pay for the damages yourself so that this matter will be closed. Now, let's see, how much was it?"

"A hundred denarius," the guards' leader said.

Natir yelped with shock, "For a broken table and a couple of chairs?"

"You are not one to decide the value of the damage," Wilhelm said, "just hurry up and pay it and let us all go home."

"Who can afford such insane amount? I might as well make new ones myself."

"What insane amount? You really expect me to believe that you don't have the money when the paint on your waist alone is worth more?"

Natir stammered, "I...I never paid for that."

"What do you mean you never paid for it?"

"It was a gift."

"And what about the expensive dress you're wearing?"

"This too was a gift...honest."

Wilhelm roared with rage, "Are you trying to take me for a fool?"

"Sire—"

"I am done with your cheap trickery, and I have exhausted my patience with you."

"Sire, I swear—"

"Don't you dare swear on lies in my face. I have given you every chance I possibly can, but if you insist on playing this kind of game with me, then I will deal with you in a very different manner."

The old guard was on his toes as he tried to gain Wilhelm's attention again. "Sire, please."

Wilhelm scoffed with impatience, "What? What is it? Can't you see what I'm dealing with here?"

The old guard spoke quietly, "Sire, I beg you, I bring urgent word: One of the slaves took their life."

"What? Slaves? What slaves?"

"From the Dog-Cage."

His eyes darted left and right. It took Wilhelm a moment for the news to sink in. "Well then, go and buy a replacement. What do you need my permission for?"

"That's what I'm trying to explain. Sire, I can't find any."

Wilhelm jumped to his feet and glared at him. "What do you mean you can't find any? This is Wenclas, we've got slaves by the masses."

"Yes, but I can't find any at this hour," said the old guard.

"You realize that it's my turn to host the event, don't you? What do you want the people to say about me? Go get some, now! Go to Adele. Go to Walcott, buy a dozen, and I don't care what the price is."

"I've already been to all of them. Sire, this isn't their hour, none of them are at their businesses."

Wilhelm buried his face in his palm.

"All right, go get a replacement from my house then," Wilhelm said, but he seemed very reluctant to go with that option and stopped the old guard right after. "B...b...but, not the redhead, I like her."

"Yes, Sire."

He stopped him again. "And not Radford, I need him."

"Yes—"

"Wait, are you absolutely sure you can't find any? I'll pay any price."

"Sire, I swear I've looked everywhere I can think of before coming here. I wouldn't have bothered you otherwise."

Hoping to gain favor in the eyes of the judge, the guards' leader joined the conversation. "This slave you've lost, was it a man or a woman?" he asked.

"A woman," said the old guard.

The guards' leader signaled the old guard to wait and pulled Wilhelm aside for a private word.

"How about that one?" the guards' leader said quietly, motioning towards Natir.

"What?" Wilhelm threw a swift glance towards Natir and back to his speaker. "But she's an outsider. The lord's orders were very clear—"

"*Relax*. She's just a tribeless runaway-slave and we all know it. An hour from now, who will remember she ever existed…? I'm only suggesting, of course. The decision is yours."

Wilhelm mulled over his words for a little while then nodded. He returned and assumed his seat.

"So, back to you," Wilhelm addressed Natir. "You say that you can neither afford to pay for the damages you caused nor prove to which clan you belong so that someone might take responsibility for your actions, did I hear you right?"

"I told you, I'm with the Toic," she responded. "Look, Sire, just send for them, send for any of them and ask."

He said with no interest and whilst cleaning his ear with his pinky, "Yes, well, I'm a little reluctant to do that now, especially after all the nonsense you spout."

"They will affirm my word!"

"Mm, if it's true, then yes, I guess they can. But if it's another sad joke, then it will only be a waste of my time. Anyway, it's getting late now, and I am very tired. So, let's call it for today and I will look into this matter again tomorrow."

A sinking sensation snuck into Natir's chest. She asked with worry, "Why tomorrow?"

Wilhelm rested his cheek on his fist and motioned with his other hand for the old guard. "Take her away."

The old guard turned his head between Natir and Wilhelm uncertainly. "You mean to the Dog-Cage?"

Wilhelm hissed, "I said, I'll look into her matter tomorrow. Now, *take her.*"

The old guard signaled a couple of their men, who approached Natir at his command.

Natir retreated. "Wait, wait just a moment."

"Come with us."

"Where? Why delay it until tomorrow? Call for them now. Hey? Hey, I'm talking to you!"

They grabbed her arms. "I said, come with us, move it."

"Stop resisting."

Natir struggled and dug her heels in as they dragged her away, screaming, "No, wait! What Dog-Cage? Stop! I didn't do anything! Stop! Send for the Toic! I'm not lying, I swear. Please listen to me! The earl, Alfred, he will tell you, ask him, ask any of them, they all know me. Please. Where are you taking me? Stop!"

Chapter 12

RELEASED

Agatha and Teyrnon were at one of the town-guards' keeps, talking to the guard they had to bribe just to inquire about Natir's fate.

"What do you mean she's not in there?" Agatha asked.

"I mean we don't have her," the guard said. "She's not here."

"She has to be."

"Did you call out her name?" asked Teyrnon.

"Look, it's not exactly a maze," the guard replied. "We have got only two halls where the arrested are being held, and I've already went through each hall twice and asked everyone, okay? There is no woman called Natir inside. Your friend must be being held somewhere else. There are two more keeps for this kind of thing, one of them is near the marketplace by—"

"We've already been to the other two," Teyrnon interrupted.

"She wasn't at either of them, this is the last place. She has to be here."

The guard waved his arms. "I don't know what else to tell you except that I did my part, and I'm certain she's not inside. I'm sorry. Perhaps you should go back to the other keeps and check with them again."

He went back inside, leaving Agatha and Teyrnon in dismay.

"What do we do now…?" Teyrnon asked. "You think we should go back to the other ones?"

"No, we can't keep running in circles like this. We must tell Alfred."

"If we tell him—"

"Then the blame is on you," she raged. "This is your fault. You caused this."

Anxiously, he said, "Look, let's just keep calm and go back to the other keeps one more time to double-check. Maybe—"

"I'm not wasting any more time or money on this."

"But she could be in trouble."

"It's already *trouble*." She raised her voice, "Look, Teyrnon, I swear to Veles, I don't care what happens to Natir or what water she sinks herself in. *But Alfred does*. And if I don't tell him right away, then I will only be letting you and Natir drag me down with you by my heels."

"No one is trying to—"

"This kind of thing can only get worse. Do you understand what I'm saying? Now, let's go. We need to tell Alfred, and he will decide what to do about this." She rushed down the street, cursing, "Where on Earth is she?"

* * *

Her wrists in bronze, Natir was thrown with her face against the wall.

She was crying with frantic pain and didn't have half a chance to resist; the guard who pushed her was at her back in an instant, entrapping her body between himself and the wall.

She stammered with half-words and wriggled against his hold for but a moment before she felt his hand squeeze against the back of her neck. The pressure forced her head still—titled hard to the back—and caused her to stand on her toes, unable to move.

"Be still," he commanded.

The hunger in his voice intimidated her. Natir submitted to his authority and did not resist as he positioned her hands high over her head.

She shut her eyes with bitterness and dug her nails against the cold bricks when he eased his weight off her and worked on the belt of her dress.

Natir had thought that the guards who brought her to this place were cruel and filthy enough, but this new guard whom they delivered her to had proved her wrong. Once his friends had left, he had wasted no time before he revealed his true colors and thrashed at her face, dealing her one slap after another until the pain was so intense that Natir couldn't collect her thoughts together enough to make sense of what was happening to her.

He undid the dress's straps at her shoulders with urgency and yanked her dress straight up over her head, but the chain at her wrists caused the tangling of her arms in the fabric.

A sharp cry escaped her mouth when he twisted her arms back. He was more worried about getting the dress off her body undamaged than he would have been if both her arms had broken in the process.

Once he freed Natir from her clothes, he twirled his chained captive defenseless in his hold as he pulled her onto himself then shoved her back against the wall and commanded, "The sandals, too."

Her shoulder battered against the bricks, and her head bumped onto the wall, causing Natir to hunch her back.

She looked up at him, baffled at first, then when she saw him folding her clothes, she realized that it was her dress he was really after.

"Do it!"

She obeyed and raised her right foot and slipped off her sandal then took off the other one and handed them over to him.

To the little her chain would allow, Natir crossed her hands at her chest and shuddered in anguished humiliation. Her slender fingers could barely cover her breasts as she stood before him with nothing left on her skin but the white scarf wrapped around her hips for a loincloth.

He went to place her clothes on a table then turned around and wildly checked her out up and down with the same letch look he had had in his eyes since the moment he laid eyes on her.

The guard approached her again, intending to strip her of the last piece of clothing she had.

Natir jolted; a repressed "No" burst from her lips, and she

quickly threw her hands down to stop him, but he treated her face with a smack that set her cheek on fire. In a flash, he lunged at her, ramming her with his whole body, and entrapped her against the wall again.

Her face turned sidewise, she shut her eyes and felt his breath against her cheek as he murmured, "Be quiet."

His eyes leered at her face hungrily, aroused by her feminine mortified expression. He brushed through her hair with one hand and reached down with the other, fondling her breast and causing her to gasp.

"This worthen some money, didn't it?" he said in a low, gleeful voice.

Emboldened by her submission, he stroked his thumb around her nipple in circles, then he savagely wrung around her breast meat with his hand and pulled and jerked it around in every way, causing Natir to hold her breath and glue her lips together not to scream with agony.

She inhaled one shuddering breath after another through her nose as he let go of her breast.

"But not as much as this…" His palm slid down her belly to the white scarf where he tucked half his forefinger between her skin and the fabric.

A sob broke clear of her lips, and she cringed in humiliation, standing at the brink of feeling him violate her flesh at any time he wished for it.

"Why wear something that cost more than your own

worth?" He toyed with her nerves, slowly running his finger sideways just above her crotch.

"Please no. Please no," she whimpered, on the verge of tears.

His hand settled on the knot to her side, intending to unwrap it, but he changed his mind at the last moment and took a few steps back.

Natir opened her eyes, only to see him snicker at her.

"Take it off," he said with a motion of his head.

She couldn't force herself to obey and begged him to stop with her eyes.

He put his hand atop the whip he had at his belt. "You know where you're at, don't you?"

His words shattered what little resistance she had left and caused Natir to drop her face with defeat.

She was no longer free. She wasn't even a slave anymore and could not find the sad refuge a property might hope to seek in her master's stature. She was their captive. Skin bare and solus to the world. Her existence had instantly become lower than that of the dogs in the streets, and there was nothing they couldn't do to her, unliable.

"Be smart."

Half a sob escaped her throat. She sniffled and wiped her nose with the back of her hand then nodded bitterly and looked back at him.

With her hands to her chest and her eyes to him, Natir bent her knees and sagged slowly onto the floor where she curled in on herself.

"That's it, strip yourself for me."

Natir held her breath, shut her eyes, and felt a warm tear run down her cheek.

She reached for the knot…

"What are you doing?"

Her face shot out towards the voice.

The tears blurred her vision. Natir blinked her eyes to try and clear them; she saw another guard standing at the room's entrance with a cup of beer in his hand.

This one was an older man with a streak of gray in his hair. His build was strong, and he had a very domineering presence. His face was firm, almost like an angry father, and his forest eyes were cold and cruel without a shred compassion in them, like that of a man long hardened by life that had seen it all a thousand times before.

"Did you steal her clothes?"

The younger guard answered, "She doesn't need it."

"Is she the replacement?"

"She is. That's what I was saying."

He motioned. "Give her her clothes back."

"No way, look at it, it's brand new." The younger guard raised the dress in the air. "This thing worth real money. It will be a waste."

The older guard shook his head. "I'll be right back. Keep your hands off her." He put his cup on a shelf and stepped out of sight for a moment.

Anxious, Natir turned her face back to the younger guard as he stared down at her.

"Stand up. Stand up, I said!"

He grabbed her chain and pulled Natir to her feet, then he suddenly thrust forward and forced himself on her, holding her around the ears and locking his lips onto hers.

Natir panicked and struggled in his grasp, trying to claw at him with her chained hands as he mashed his dry lips against hers.

"What did I just tell you?" the older guard shouted. He had returned to the room with a small roll of old, gray clothes in his hands.

The moment Natir managed to free herself, she snarled and dropped herself onto the floor, spitting and panting for air.

"What?" the younger guard asked, frustrated. "Can't anyone have a little bit of a good time around here, it's all work or what?"

"You are disgusting." The older guard approached them. "Who is so gross, he would have sex with someone and glare at their insides an hour later?"

"It's not like—" Before the younger guard could finish, he was pushed out of the way by his friend.

"I don't care what you think," the older guard barked at him and threw the clothes he had brought onto Natir's arms without looking at her. "This is my post. Only what I think matters. And I say it's disgusting, and you're disgusting, and this shouldn't be how it ends for anybody."

The younger guard still tried to object.

"Not a word," the older guard silenced him. "You wanted the dress? The dress is yours. But that's it. *Don't push it any further.*" He grabbed Natir's arm and pulled her up. "You, come with me."

The older guard led Natir to a hallway just around the door.

It was a narrow passage and somewhat dark, built with bricks, and had eight or ten holding cells on either side sealed with bronze bars.

"Thank you," she said in a small voice, but he didn't offer her a mere glance in return.

He opened one of the holding cells and instructed, "Put the clothes on and get inside."

She motioned with her chained hands in response.

He huffed with vexation, took one of the two pieces of clothes, and wrapped it around her bare chest.

The older guard's eyes, tone, and touch simply lacked any sexual desire. Natir didn't feel embarrassed to hold herself still for him and let him work on her freely.

"You can put on the other one yourself. Now, get in."

Natir hoped she could find in this man a savior, so she obeyed his orders in deference and walked inside. She clung to the bars and pleaded to him whilst he worked on the lock.

"Sir, may I please ask you for something? Sir…? Sir, wait!"

Deaf to her words, he left unbothered.

Natir dropped her forehead against the bars, shut her eyes, and let out a great breath. She then wiped the traces of her tears off with her palms and turned towards the voice coming from within the holding cell…

She had to keep her knees slightly bent and could not stand at full height due to the low ceiling.

The holding cell was constructed from bricks in the form of an arch. It was barely five feet in height and just as much in width, but it extended a good thirty or forty feet inwards, which made it look more like a tunnel.

The place was at its darkest on the inside as there were no torches, and she caught the foul scent of mold and human urine coming from within. It made staying where she was, next to the entrance, much more feasible to Natir.

She searched the dark with her eyes and recognized the shape of the only other person imprisoned in the cell with her. It was a woman who had curled in on herself and was sobbing quietly.

Natir tied the second piece of clothing around her hips for a skirt then sat next to the bars with her eyes nailed to the woman.

"Hello… My name is Natir…… What's your name?"

The woman didn't respond.

Natir tilted her head back and exhaled a sigh. She couldn't blame the woman for ignoring her. Natir herself was reeling under so much stress by then that she wasn't sure she could make a proper conversation no matter how badly she wanted some answers. She needed a moment just to pull herself together first.

She dropped her face in her hands, thinking about the disastrous situation she had ended up in.

The sound of a clang next to her feet made Natir jolt from surprise. She had been so lost in thought that she hadn't noticed the older guard return until he was pushing a cup of beer and a quarter loaf of bread hemmed with bite-marks through the bars.

Natir hastened to her feet and pleaded again. "Sir, Sir, please listen to me, I need your help, I need to get a word out to someone. Sir? Sir, will you please—"

He huffed and said, unruly, "Will you be quiet?"

"I need your help."

He raised his hand for Natir to stop talking.

"How many times do you think I have to hear this every night?" he said. "I'm sorry, and that's all that I can offer you: my sympathy. I can't do anything for you. I can't pull any favors to no one. And none of this is my call to begin with. I'm just the man doing work no one else wants, try to understand that... Sit down, eat something, and try not to think about it."

Natir called out as he turned to leave, "What did you mean by what you said earlier?"

He stopped. "What did I say earlier?"

"You asked your friend: who wants to have sex with someone only to glare at their insides an hour later? What did you mean by that?"

He frowned and stared back at her for a little pause as he realized that Natir had no clue where she was.

"Perhaps it's for the best that you don't know." He then motioned at the food. "Now, eat something. There's beer, too."

As he disappeared behind the door, Natir sat down and pulled on her bangs as she resigned herself to the secrecy and bane he had left her with.

She reached for the food but then decided to give it another shot at starting a conversation with the other woman.

Natir wriggled on her hips and turned a bit more towards the woman, tilted her head to one side, and faked a smile. "I'm not really into drinking right now," she said softly. "Would you like to have some?"

The woman wiped her tears off. She pulled herself together and walked tiredly towards Natir.

She was a slave with short black hair and had the marks of many masters tattooed to her neck and upper half. She wasn't that young or even a good looker. In fact, there was little about her casual looks to compliment her for, and the bitter crying had taken its toll on her face.

"Here." Natir offered her the cup.

To Natir's surprise, the woman took it with both hands and did not let go of the cup until she drank it all. She didn't seem thirsty or even to be liking the taste of it, but just desperate for the liquor to do its work on her.

Natir wiped the vexed look off her face and faked a smile again. "What's your name?"

Before the woman could choose whether or not to answer, they heard the sound of footsteps approaching their cell. It caused the woman to spin on her heel towards the entrance with terror in her eyes.

"What's wrong?" Natir was perplexed at the woman trembling from head to toe and stealing steps backwards with her eyes nailed to the door. She was panting so hard that she looked like she was choking.

Natir looked over her shoulder at the older guard opening the lock with two men at his flank.

"They sent you a replacement?" one man asked.

"Yes. Tell them they don't need to stall anymore."

"Understood. We're down to the last two anyway."

The men came inside. One of them reached for Natir as she was the closest to the door.

"No," the older guard said. "This one just got here, give her a break, let her finish her meal first."

The man nodded in return and motioned instead at the other woman. "All right, let's go."

The woman's legs betrayed her. She fell to her knees, covered her mouth, and sobbed.

"Let's go."

"You're going to cause trouble?"

The woman dropped her face, crying, then nodded her head and walked out.

Natir's chest heaved with worry.

"Where are you taking her?" she asked from where she sat as the guard worked on the lock. "What is this place? I was told I'm supposed to see the judge again tomorrow."

He ignored her and addressed the men instead as they led the other woman away, "No more stalling, you hear me? Let's just get it done with and we can all go home."

"Where am I? What's going to happen to her? Will you please answer me?"

He mumbled, halfway to the door, "She's released."

Natir couldn't believe a word he said. If anything, it only made her feel worse.

Chapter 13

TAKEN

Alfred slammed his hand down and the table rattled under his palm.

"Natir was what?" He glared at them like a demon in the forking flames.

Agatha and Teyrnon cohered together, nabbed by his glare.

"It is...as we told you."

"The town guards have her," Agatha said. "We know that for sure, we just don't know where they took her."

"We searched everywhere, but it's confusing and no one seems to know her whereabouts for sure."

"AND YOU WAITED THIS LONG TO TELL ME?" he roared, startling them both to their toes.

"Who's Natir?" Bertwin asked.

Alfred turned his head back and forth between Bertwin and the two. The interruption had given him the breather he needed to calm down before he could go overboard.

"Wait for me outside," he told them then turned to Bertwin. "I'm afraid we'll have to cut this reunion short, Bertwin. I have another matter to attend."

Bertwin looked up at Alfred, who had gotten off his seat.

"We haven't settled the matter at hand yet."

"There is nothing to settle. You have shared your mind, and I did, too. The rest is just how things will unfold."

Bertwin frowned and gave a low grunt as he stared at Alfred's back, who walked out the hospitality house with his men abandoning their tables and flocking behind him.

"Father?" Antigone approached Bertwin and said with a childish whine when he turned his face to her, "How much longer will you keep me waiting?"

The frown wouldn't let go of his face easily. "Ah, sorry, my dear." He pat her head then called, "Fedor. Go with your sister, Antigone, and buy her whatever she wants."

She grabbed his sleeve. "But I want you to come."

"Later, my dear." He kissed her forehead. "It looks like I have urgent business to take care of."

"Let's go, Antigone," said Fedor.

"Go with your brother now. Go. I'll catch up with you soon, I promise."

As his children left, two of Bertwin's men approached him.

"What do we do now?" one of them said.

"Your friend has turned us down, Bertwin. We wasted a day waiting for the Toic for nothing."

"No," said Bertwin, "Alfred will change course for sure, and things will go exactly as we hope."

"How? You've been trying to convince him for an hour."

Bertwin smirked and looked between his men and the door from which Alfred had left.

"The best thing about having friends is not the swords they bring to your side," he said. "It's the barred confidences they so easily open up to you with... Alfred's biggest weakness are these *women* he thinks so much of. They fascinate him, and there is absolutely nothing that he will not do for them. And I've got the feeling that one of them has just landed herself in a tight spot."

Bertwin then motioned for one of the men to hand him a cup of wine and ordered, "Get me Hagen and Vadim at once. They know this town better than anyone else, and their friends here are many and resourceful."

"I'll go get them."

"What would you have them do?" his man asked.

"Turn the town upside-down if they have to. We need to be quick and find out who and where *thisss* Natir might be. And we must get our hands on her before Alfred does... Right now, she is the key to control the Toic."

* * *

Alfred met with Agatha and Teyrnon outside.

One man asked, "We are still leaving in the morning, right?"

Alfred look at him. "Yes. Go make sure that everyone is where they should be. We leave at first light."

His man motioned a couple of their friends and headed out to carry out his task.

"We—"

Before Teyrnon could ask, Alfred answered, "But I'm not leaving this town without Natir."

Agatha took a step in and asked, "How do you want us to do this?"

Teyrnon followed, "We can send riders. Have them check with the keeps again and other places the town guards have that we didn't have a chance to look at."

"No," Alfred said. "If this town has her, then there's only one thing to do: We'll go straight to the man on top."

* * *

Quietly and with worry written on her face, the servant stood next to Hallstein's bed, keeping an eye on her.

"How is she?"

She turned around and saw Alediya enter the room.

"Not well," the servant responded under her breath.

Alediya came next to her. She took the cloth from the servant's hand, knelt by the bed, and wiped the sweat off Hallstein's face with it as Hallstein twisted and turned in her sleep.

"It was the same the night before." The servant added with pity in her voice, "She kept turning in her sleep... At times, she mumbled something, I don't know what, I couldn't make out the words."

"Same dream? The wolf in chains again?"

"I don't know."

"You didn't ask?"

"I did, but she wouldn't say."

Alediya sighed. She wet the cloth from a nearby pot and wiped Hallstein's face and neck with it once more. "Did you give her the sleeping potion?"

"She became hysterical when I offered it to her. She cried, broke a few plates, and threw her mirror at me. She said she would rather die than fall asleep again—"

"Did, you, give it to her or not?"

She frowned. "She's asleep, isn't she? We did as you ordered us and polluted her food with it."

Alediya shot her with a glare, and the servant backed off.

"I'm sorry," the servant said. "I chose my words poorly."

"Very poorly."

"Forgive me, it's just that I feel bad for her."

"There is nothing to feel bad about." Alediya resumed her work. "We are only doing what is best for her."

"Yes, but not like this."

"Not like what?"

"*This.* You didn't see how she was. You didn't see how afraid she was. It's like...it's like we're imprisoning her in a room with her worst fears and she can never hope to escape from it. Alediya...Alediya, it's Hallstein, for Morana's sake! Her spirit is too tender, she's not cut out for something like this."

"If you can't handle it, then leave," Alediya raised her voice with anger.

"I didn't say—"

"Or leave this house all together…" she threatened, not looking back at the servant. "Hallstein needs her sleep, just as everyone else. Now go, I'll take it over from here."

"Please."

"You are relieved for tonight," she said firmly.

The servant dropped her face. She left the room and shut the door behind her.

"Hallstein…" Alediya whispered.

She patted the young woman's forehead with the palm of her old hand as Hallstein panted for air and turned in her sleep, her arms infrequently thrown about with anxiety and her light nightdress drenched in her sweat like a woman in fever.

"What has gotten into you, my love…? What is it that your dreams are showing you?"

*   *   *

Natir killed time toying with the piece of bread and thinking about what had just happened, trying to settle on an assumption, but her thoughts were pitch-dark no matter which angle she viewed her situation from.

Before long, the men had returned. Natir stood before the door, and like she had expected, they ordered her to come out, so she did and didn't say anything.

The men flanked her from both sides and held Natir by her upper arms as they led her away.

Natir stole a look over her shoulder at the older guard, who quietly collected the cup and the piece of bread from the floor and didn't bother to close the door.

They led Natir down a long and cold corridor that soon began to descend and then rose upwards again; the farther they went, the louder the hype was, and the more anxious Natir became.

Something caught her eye.

Natir looked down as she walked and saw a rich trail of blood by her side, spreading like a carpet on the floor from one door they had just passed by to wherever the men were leading her.

Her chest began to heave with anxiety and her head shot forward when she noticed two men heading in the opposite direction, dragging something behind them.

Suddenly, a shudder ran down her spine and caused Natir to forget how to breathe.

They were dragging the woman she had been held captive with, by her ankles.

She was still alive, Natir could see the woman's body twitch weakly as she gargled her last breaths. Her body was disfigured, marked with cuts and missing chunks of flesh all over, and her throat was ripped open with bubbles of blood bursting out of her neck as she tried to breathe.

The hysteria took the best of Natir. She tried to escape her captors and screamed, "Hey! HEY, WAIT. NO. WHAT IS THIS?"

One man quickly grabbed her by her upper arm and the chain in her hands as the other man got a hold of her other hand and hair to restrain her, "Keep moving."

"STOP, STOP!"

"I said keep moving!" The men dragged her forth.

"I've got her, I've got her."

"NO. I'M NOT GOING. HELP! WHERE ARE YOU TAKING ME? STOP! STOP, I SAID, STOP!"

Chapter 14

DOG-CAGE

A fever of fear.

Beads of cold sweat ran down Hallstein's skin. Her breaths were chaotic. Her dress and silver bangs had become so moist that they adhered to her skin, and a frown formed on her kind face as her head was thrown left and right.

"Donun...trovoz...den wulf...donun—"

Alediya frowned, unable to make out the words Hallstein was mumbling.

She slowly leaned her head down on the bed right next to Hallstein's and turned her ear to the young woman's lips, listening carefully.

"Donun...trovoz...letten pass......"

Hallstein then went silent. Her body lay perfectly still, and her hands subconsciously balled into fists, grasping the sheets in her fragile fingers.

"ts herein...ts herein—"

"It's here?"

She suddenly let out such a scream the likes of which Alediya couldn't believe, and her body jerked up and down in seizure.

Alediya was thrown backwards on the floor, frightened out of her mind and staring at Hallstein with eyes widened in terror.

"Hallstein…? Hallstein?" She hurried back to her, shaking Hallstein by her shoulders. "HALLSTEIN?"

The two servants barged into the room, and one of them shouted, "What happened?"

Alediya hysterically said, "She's not…she's not breathing, Hallstein?" She spun around. "GO GET HELP. CALL SOMEONE. WHICH POTION DID YOU GIVE HER? GO GET HELP NOW!"

The looks on the servants' faces alerted Alediya. They were both frozen with shock.

She turned around, slowly, following their gaze.

"Hallstein…?"

* * *

Natir put a desperate struggle to stop the men from dragging her any farther.

She cursed, and she screamed, and she glued her bare feet to the floor and squirmed in their grasp to try and escape, but it was all to no avail. The more she strained, the harder they held her.

A third guard hurried out to aid his friends; they ganged up on Natir and had to practically carry her out of the corridor and to one entrance of the grand hall.

One man uttered a wild shriek when Natir bit his hand, but his cry was lost amidst the magnificent bellow of the hall.

"Bitch!"

In his rage, he threw Natir squirming free onto the floor, behind a short wooden fence.

Hardly anyone noticed what was happening behind that fence where Natir curled in on herself in the fetal position and covered her face with her arms as two of the men vented their anger on her, kicking her on the floor.

They beat her so veraciously and treated her limbs with their sticks until she wished she had never resisted.

One man pulled her halfway upwards by her hair and landed an unrestrained slap to her face that sent Natir tumbling downward like a rock. She lay flat against the floor, and he stomped on her head and threatened to kill her if she tried anything.

Despite her submission and tearful reply, he didn't take his shoe off her head before giving it a twist, mashing her ear under his heel and causing Natir to scream and her body to jerk in agony.

They pulled Natir to her feet, entrapped her between them, and ordered her to stay still.

Natir sniffled and wiped her watery eyes with her hand and tried to reach for her ear, which felt like it was on fire, but the man slapped her hands down before she could.

She blinked back tears and glanced left and right.

It was such a mesmerizing sight…

The hall was a very large, oval-shaped structure with no pillars towards the center at all. Not a single nail had been used to build it. Whole tree trunks were interlocked in a brilliant design to make the roof hold itself together, as if this gigantic heavy mass hovering overhead were floating in the air.

Beneath it, rows of benches were laid out in sharp spirals descending to create an amphitheater overlooking the stage below where a round bronze cage—three hundred fifty feet in diameter and fifteen feet in height—stood.

The cage was embellished by bronze firepits carried in the arms of life-sized copper statues of nude maidens scattered about, bathing the sand and every inch of the stage with their firelight and causing the cage bars to shine like blood-glazed gold.

On the ground level, nine incredible entrances made of engraved wood in the shape of gigantic jaws led to the nine doors of the cage, at one of which Natir was being held.

Hundreds of people crowded the hall, maybe even a thousand. They were cramped closely together and behaved so tempestuously that they created a din the likes of which a thousand beehives would fail to match.

A sharp scream rattled her heart.

Inside the cage, Natir saw a man getting attacked by a dog that bit his arm right below the wrist.

The man desperately fought back. He kept his back to the bars as he kicked and punched at the dog with his bare hands, but then a second dog appeared out of nowhere, and the man was fatally overwhelmed. Then came a third, and a fourth.

He bled from head to toe in no time and was repeatedly knocked down to his knee only to rush back up with hysteria, knowing that to embrace the ground meant his death. In his panic, he tried to run away and had managed to run but a few steps before he was knocked down onto his back with a resounding scream, and the hungry beasts quickly gathered over him.

The horrific sight bewitched Natir and caused her chest to heave with panic.

He was crying for help, and not a trace of him could be seen but his wriggling blood-soaked arms as the pack of dogs dragged him left and right, rending at his limbs.

A dog leapt the other way, and Natir's hands flew to her mouth with a loud gasp. She could see into the man's body.

The flesh of his waist was ripped off whole, and soon his guts scattered onto the ground as he was thrown the other way, alive, and the show was yet to end.

The crowed had gone hysterical with excitement and all that Natir could hear them say was a jumble of a few words: colors!

Some yelled "Yellow," others screamed for "Red," "Blue," "Orange," "Green," "Violet," and "Light-blue."

A motion stole her eyes.

Natir's face darted towards a stand that was set up a few arm's-lengths above ground level at one side of the cage, for pellucid view at the scene below.

Three persons staged it. One of them was an overly dressed man with an official appearance who paid his whole attention to the struggle unfolding below.

The other was a midget with a comical custom. He had a horn full of water set on the table in front of him. The horn dripped from its bottom onto a small wooden basin hung by strings. Once the basin was full, it would flip over, empty its contents, and flip upwards again.

The device was set for a very short time, to the count of ten, and the midget was adding to the thrill by tapping his palms to a table, urging it to run faster.

Next to him was a beautiful young woman with rich, long, wavy blonde hair to be envied for. She was dressed for captivation, and the darling blue in her eyes was a siren to the souls of men.

Once the basin flipped, the woman would reach her hand to a silver pot and pick a stick with a color painted at its concealed end.

She would raise it high in her arm for everyone to see and spin around with a charming smile while the midget jumped up and down, calling the color.

"Violet! Violet! Violet!"

At his cry, another door was opened and a dog with a violet scarf wrapped around its collar shot into the scene, barking with randiness to join the murdering.

One of the dogs sank its fangs into the man's throat and stole a chunk of his flesh in its jaw.

The overly dressed man—the gamekeeper—rang his bell and declared aloud the color of the winning dog, and the woman picked the right stick from the ones she had in her hand and, again, she raised it for all to see, causing the hall to erupt with jeers and victorious cries alike.

The woman laughed and blew her kisses into the air, saluting the winners, and the coins of gratuities fell from all around her, showering the ground from above.

The terror unfolding before her eyes caused Natir's thoughts to fragment; it was as if fear had wreathed her mind like smoke.

Natir had finally grasped the true gravity of the danger dressing her, and it was much, much worse than anything she could have expected.

The people were waging their bets on which of the seven dogs would thrust the killing bite onto the entrapped prey's throat. And she was the next prey.

"Veles…have mercy."

Natir was entangled in the web of a game of life and death, the likes of which she could never hope to triumph. She was going to have to fight for her life all alone, unarmed and skin-bare to the world.

Her foes were a thousand men gone mad with letch, seven blood-thirsty beasts, each her own size and trained to kill, and thirty of the swords of authority.

And from behind them loomed all the power and majesty of the great throne of Wenclas.

* * *

Hallstein's chest heaved steadily in and out, sending gasps onto her lips.

Her body had turned stiff as wood, and her eyes were wide open and staring still at the ceiling, yet she was not conscious nor blinking, as though she were possessed.

"This isn't normal," one servant stammered with fear.

"What happened to her? Alediya? Alediya, what do we do?"

Alediya approached the bed carefully and reached out her hand, but fear caused her to draw it back halfway through.

"Hallstein…? Can you hear me?"

Hallstein's head suddenly dropped to one side, staring at Alediya with lidless eyes and causing Alediya to startle and stumble a step back.

The pink lips twisted, and in a rasping voice, she said with a language unheard of to the world.

"Don't provoke the wolf…"

* * *

The slaves skimmed off the shattered remains of the last victim, and the men dragged Natir forth into the cage.

Natir screamed and struggled with panic and held on to the bars when they opened the door, refusing to be forced inside.

One man teared at her fingers as Natir shot her legs at him, whilst the other pulled Natir by the waist and finally managed to throw her into the cage.

"No! Stop, stop!" With sand taunting her mouth, Natir hurried to her feet and ran back to them, but they had already shut and locked the door in her face.

She shook the door and shouted, "LET ME OUT, LET ME OUT OF HERE!"

"Give me your hands," one guard raised his voice, causing Natir to freeze. "You want to do this in chains? Hurry up and give me your hands."

It took a moment for his words to make sense to Natir. She thrust her hands through the bars, and the guard worked on her wrists.

"With this, we conclude the last of the males' fight. Congratulations to all winners," the gamekeeper declared, then pointed out the blonde woman with his arm. "Don't forget to tip your hosts and, above all, the beauty to whom you owe your luck."

The blonde woman spun around and waved her arm to the audience as the cheers and commotion rose to a deafening hype.

Natir's face shot towards the gamekeeper and back to the guard. She begged with haste, "Please, please, I have a daughter. Please let me out of here, this is a mistake, I'm not a slave, I'm not supposed to be here—"

"And now, we're down to the last of the female contenders. May the best of luck be with all of you."

The guard removed Natir's chains and suddenly held on firmly to her wrists. "I'll tell you one thing—"

She looked back at him with panic in her eyes and gave his words her full attention.

"Go for yellow."

Jaw dropped, Natir couldn't trust her ears. "What?"

"Go for yellow, yellow. I bet everything I've got on it."

The shock left Natir speechless. She couldn't believe what the man was asking from her nor how dead-serious he was about it.

"You're going to die anyway, might as well do me this favor, one last deed—"

"The fuck if I will!" she shouted as she teared her hands from his grip and ran the other way.

She raced towards the opposite door where the last victim had been dragged through and shook at its bars, but it was shut solid.

Her back to the bars, Natir turned her face left and right searching for an escape that was never there. Her chest heaved like mad, and her knees knocked together for how frightened she had become.

Natir undid her skirt in a hurry and with trembling hands wrapped it on her left forearm, preparing for what's coming, all while the crowd above deafened her ears with their calls.

Every one of them was asking her to die, to offer her throat to this dog or the other for their sake.

She couldn't take it. Her chest was filled with hate.

"HAVE YOU ALL RUN AMUCK?" She turned her face up towards them and shouted with all her voice, as wild as a woman could be, "Have your hearts fallen apart?!"

Her cry caused the hype to tone down greatly, but not entirely, as many paid her mind.

"Who throws their living slaves to the dogs like this? What rotten wombs bred people like you? A thousand times I curse you, and to rubble Perun thunders your homes!"

The crowd booed with pride, anger, and shock, and some of them threw trash at her.

*   *   *

"—Don't provoke it."

*   *   *

The blonde woman had raised an eyebrow as she listened to Natir.

She smirked, pushed the midget out of her way, and did not wait for the gamekeeper to call the next game to reach for the pot and pick herself a stick.

She raised it high in the air and shouted, "Punish the curser!"

And the midget hopped with thrill.

"Red! Red! Red!"

To be continued…

Thank You!

I hope you enjoyed a good read and that you will choose to share this experience with your friends

& don't miss out on the chance to tell the world what you think, by posting your review on Amazon!

Coming next,

Book III of the series

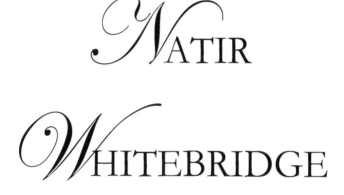

NATIR

WHITEBRIDGE

For all enquiries please contact the author at:
James.Starvoice@gmail.com

Printed in Great Britain
by Amazon